ALATHIA PARIS MORGAN

Ding Dong! Is She Dead?

Nova Ladies Adventures Book #1

To my brother, Micah. Since you went to heaven, I realized that life is short, so you are the reason that this book got finished. You may have gotten to heaven first, but I wrote the first book. Miss you tons...

To my readers. Thank you for the inspirational ideas that have inspired the creation of this fictional book. You are truly awesome.

This is a work of fiction and in no way is meant to portray actual people, names, places, events or situations. The ideas were from the author's own imagination and any resemblance to people living or dead is entirely coincidental.

Copyright: 2014 Alathia Morgan

Second Edition: June 2015

Third Edition: April 2017

All rights reserved. No part of this book may be used or reproduced in any manner without written permission, except in the case of quotations for articles and reviews.

Acknowledgements: Thanks so much to my editor; I couldn't have done it without you. Rebel Edits & Designs

Maria Weaver, Gerree Bollum, Pam Geske, and Mom, who all took the time to read this and give your opinions.

Book cover: All credit with the book cover design goes to Nicole Paris, thank you. You Rock!!

Dreamstime photos for the cover photo.

Jennifer stepped out the back door of the bar, bracing the door open with her foot as she carried the bags of trash to the dumpster. Throwing the bags inside, she turned to go back inside, but stopped when she heard hushed voices arguing.

"Joe, lift it higher." A tall man groaned under the weight of the bundle in his arms.

"Shut up, Freddie. I've got the heavy side, you've got the feet," Joe retorted, heaving his end higher to lift it over the edge of the trunk.

Curiosity overcame her good sense. When she peeked around the dumpster, she saw two men trying to lift a man into the back of a black Lincoln Town Car. She watched with growing horror as they struggled to place a body in the trunk.

Freddie shoved his end into the large space, but when he tried to slam the trunk shut, it hit the body's foot and it popped open again, hitting him in the head.

"What the hell?" Joe exclaimed, walking back toward the trunk. "No wonder it wouldn't close, you moron. You left his shoe hanging out." The street light was directly on Freddie's face, and if looks could kill, Joe would be dead.

Stifling a giggle, Jennifer ducked back into the shadows as the two men climbed inside the car and drove past the dumpster she was hiding behind.

Crime dramas always said that the license plate number was important, so she repeated it to herself as she waited for the taillights to fade out of sight.

She glanced around as she crept back inside the bar.

With shaking hands, she managed to lock the door behind her, then collected her purse and jacket as she went to the front.

"Ted, I'm ready to leave if you could let me out."

"Sure. Let me turn out the rest of the lights." Ted moved to the breaker on the wall. Flipping switches, the room became engulfed in darkness. The only illumination in the building was from the red exit sign above the door. She jumped when Ted walked up behind her, with his keys in hand.

"Oh, you startled me. Don't sneak up on a girl like that," she said, playfully hitting his arm. "You ready?"

Ted grunted his response as she held the door open.

Making sure no one was hanging around, Ted locked the door and turned. "Bye, Jennifer. See you tomorrow," he muttered, heading in the opposite direction.

Waiting until Ted was out of sight, she made her way to the police station down the street.

The precinct was loud and busy as she stepped up to the front desk. "Sir, I need to report a crime." She wrapped her knuckles on the counter, hoping to gain his attention.

Barely glancing up from his report, he took in her bar attire. "Sure, lady. Have a seat and someone will be with you in a little while." He motioned her to a bench filled with handcuffed drunks waiting to be processed.

Preferring to stand by the wall, downwind of the drunks, she waited patiently for twenty minutes before her anger got the best of her.

She walked back up to the desk and asked in a firm voice, "Is there someone who would be able to take my statement about a crime I witnessed?"

"Just wait over there by the wall and we'll get to you when we can." He dismissed her again as he turned away to answer the phone, unconcerned with her problem.

Using the wall to hold her weight, she waited for another frustrating fifteen minutes, and decided she would give the police one more chance before leaving.

"Excuse me!" Jennifer yelled out. "Can someone help me out? I need to report a crime, if you're not too busy to solve one!"

A passing detective heard her and came toward the desk to help. "Miss, why don't you come over here to my desk and explain what's going on." He waved the desk sergeant away. "I've got this.

Following the detective through a maze of desks, she stopped as he cleaned out a chair.

"Hi, I'm Detective Banner. What can I do for you, Ms...?" he asked as he took the seat across from her.

"Oh, sorry. I'm Jennifer Smith. It sure is crazy here on Saturday nights." She reached out to shake his offered hand. "I think someone was murdered."

"You were saying you have a crime to report, and now it's a murder?" He looked at her intently, trying to decide if she was just another crazy lady, or if she really had witnessed a crime being committed. "Which is it?" he questioned.

"I understand you probably hear all sorts of stories, especially this late at night," she apologized. "But I was taking the trash out from the bar as we were closing when I heard hushed, angry voices."

"Which bar would that be?"

"The Tiger's Bar, over on Suffolk Street, between East Houston and Stanton. This was in the alley behind the bar." Detective Banner shook his head, then motioned for her to continue.

"I watched from around the dumpster, not sure if I should get involved. Two men walked to the trunk of a car, carrying a body between them." Expecting a question, she paused.

"A body? You're sure about that?"

"Yes, sir. It certainly looked like a body. When it hit the back of the trunk with a thud, they tried to close the lid, only it wouldn't shut because a shoe was sticking out."

Jennifer tried to suppress the giggle she felt rising up by smiling. "Kind of hard to believe, I know. I thought it was funny at the time, which is why I thought it had to be real since at two a.m., there aren't many film crews hanging around alleys."

"Did you see anything else?" The detective needed a little more information. "Height? Age or race?"

"Not really. The guy named Freddie was carrying the feet, and he was taller than Joe. Joe had the heavy end, and I didn't get a look at his face. Freddie was white, with dark brown hair, or maybe it was black. He could've been Italian or Russian, but he was definitely from New York with that accent. I didn't see anything else because they drove off."

Watching the detective glance around, she quickly interjected, "I also have the license plate number if that helps, and type of car for you." Seeing a Post-it notepad and a pen on the desk, she grabbed them to write the number down as she muttered it to herself to make sure she had it right.

"That all?" he questioned again.

"I believe so. I don't remember anything else. I was hiding so they couldn't see me and put me in the trunk as well," she said, half-joking.

"All right, miss. If you'll write your name and information on this card for me, you can go."

Once she was finished filling it out, she asked, "So, what happens now?"

"We'll run the plate and look at the shops where they could have come from against the two names you mentioned. Go home and get some sleep. If we have any questions, we'll call you." Standing up, the detective dismissed her. "Thank you for reporting this, and we'll take care of it. Have a good night."

Jennifer wondered if it was just her imagination as she made her way home. *Had there been a body in the trunk?* She questioned herself. She didn't know where the information would lead, or if they would even check it out, but at least he heard her out.

She was exhausted. Maybe after a good night's sleep, she would forget all about it.

~~~

A loud pounding woke her up. Realizing it was her door, she stumbled from the bedroom, rubbing her bleary eyes as she made her way to the door where the pounding resumed.

"Hold on, I'm coming." She peered through the peephole to find two people standing in the hallway, holding up badges.

"What can I do you for?" she asked through the door.

"We're looking for a Jennifer Smith? We need to talk to her," the gentleman in the suit answered.

Swiping a tired hand over her face, she looked again to be sure she wasn't dreaming. Walking over to the counter, she picked up her phone, along with a card.

"Can I call someone to verify who you are?" She glanced at the card the detective had given her the night before.

"Detective Banner suggested you give him a call if you had any questions," the woman replied.

Jennifer dialed the number, hoping the detective was still on duty. "Yes, may I speak with Detective Banner, please? Detective Banner? Sir, I have two people outside my door who said you sent them over to talk to me. The FBI? What the hell is going on? They're here to protect me? All right, I'll make sure they're the ones you sent over, but I don't see any danger. Yes, sir. I'll see you shortly. Thank you. Bye."

"Can you tell me your names?" Jennifer held her hand over the locks, ready to open up the door. She was pretty certain at this point that they were legit.

"Agents Tombs and Riley, miss. We need to get you somewhere safe." Neither one of them were smiling as she opened the door to let them inside.

"I'll only need a minute to get dressed." She sensed they were trying to be intimidating as she moved toward her room, trying not to let their stares bother her.

"Certainly. I just need to make sure you're the only person in there." Agent Riley followed Jennifer into her bedroom and did a sweep of the bathroom. "All clear. Go ahead, miss. I'll wait outside your door."

"Um, okay?" She was a little disturbed that they were taking this so seriously. After closing the door, she dressed quickly.

Going back into her bedroom, she found Agent Riley standing in her closet, pulling clothes out and placing them into a bag on the bed. "What are you doing with my stuff?" Jennifer marched over and closed the suitcase with a thud.

"We've been told to take you to a safe place and to pack a bag, as you might not be returning." Agent Tombs answered mechanically from the doorway.

"So it *was* a body. Someone *was* murdered. Who was it?" Jennifer sank to the bed as the reality of what she had seen began to sink in.

"We're not exactly sure what's happening, but we were told to have you pack a suitcase," Agent Riley answered without sympathy.

She placed her head in her hands. "This can't be happening. I mean, I went to work yesterday, just like any other day, and now I'm leaving my home with two FBI agents for my protection."

~~~

Several days later, Jennifer was signing the paperwork that would change her life forever...

Chapter 1

Two years of bouncing around from state to state can certainly change a person, Allie thought as she looked in the mirror at her new haircut. They had finally settled her in Texas a few months ago, in hopes it would be permanent.

"Wow, I look so different. I'm glad I made the decision to go back to a more natural color." Allie shook her blonde, bobbed hair, enjoying the lightness of her new short do. "A new name and dye job certainly changes one's appearance, especially since it made me look washed out." Studying it from the side, she frowned as she looked down and realized her hair wasn't the only difference in her body.

"All this fried food since moving to the South has made my bones disappear. I actually look like a woman instead of a girl." While Allie's curves may have filled out, turning her figure into that of an attractive woman, there still weren't any men knocking on her door. The loneliness of her situation left an empty hole that she had no idea how to fill, except to throw herself into her job.

"Time to go and punch a time clock again. Why couldn't they give me a rich lifestyle when they sent me into witness protection?" Unwilling to contemplate the absence of common sense in the system for the millionth time, Allie left her one bedroom apartment.

As with many things in Texas she had discovered, everything was bigger, including apartment space. Compared to her small compact apartment in New York, her new apartment was quite spacious.

Opening the door to walk outside, Allie paused and rethought her choice of clothing as she felt the heat ready to melt a candle at seven a.m. Leaving her jacket draped over the couch, she closed the door and headed toward her ten-year-old Toyota. It was the best the agency could supply her at the moment.

"It's no Lincoln Town Car, but at least the air-conditioning still works. Who would've thought I'd need it in February?" Waving to the elderly neighbor walking the dog, Allie's adjustment to a small town included trying to be friendly to everyone around her all the time. She had to make sure she fit in, or they would relocate her again.

Driving the short distance to work, she got stuck at the light behind a trailer of live cows. "Ugh! Those things need a bath. No! Don't pee on my car! Aim it the other direction!" She waved her hands and yelled, but with the windows up, the cows didn't even glance in her direction.

~~~

"I should be thankful the cows were in a trailer and not running free," Allie mused as she pulled into the mall parking lot, where everything a rural community needed fashion-wise could be found.

Walking through the mall to her job at Balls for All Occasions, Allie passed craft stores, music stores, and the high fashion store of Bootsies Western Wear. The store was stocked with boots and hats for every occasion a cowgirl could possibly need.

Adjusting to the absence of name brand stores, like Louis Vitton or Prada, wasn't the worst challenge this Yankee had to acclimate to, but some days it seemed almost wrong.

Allie's job consisted of selling sports equipment, shoes, and clothing for every sport needed year-round to families and school athletes.

Unlocking the gate, she slid under it and closed it as she punched in the security code to shut off the alarm. Following her morning routine, she quickly had the store open for business as the clock hit the hour.

After three months at her job, Allie had a few regular customers, but today, a couple she'd never seen before walked into her store.

"What can I help you find today?" Ever the saleswoman, Allie was always helpful.

"Well, we're looking for walking or jogging shoes to start exercising together since he's retiring next week." Squeezing her husband's hand with a smile, she asks, "Can you help us find something?"

"Absolutely. Let's start over here. You can both pick out two pairs to try on and we can work from there. Is there a price range you want to stay in?" Selling shoes was not Allie's favorite part of the job, but this couple was really sweet in the way they treated each other so lovingly.

"Being comfortable is the first requirement. I don't want to get blisters when we're trying to get in shape."

A few styles later, the couple were happy with their finds and ready to pay, when the woman startled Allie at the checkout.

"Honey, did you know you can make a commission on helping people just like you did with us today?"

The woman reached into her purse and pulled out a business card, along with her money. Plastered across the front were the words, *"You can start your own career today!"*

Trying not to be rude, Allie picked up her money to finish the transaction, leaving the card on the counter. "I have a great job here. I've been here almost three months now, and my boss is wonderful."

"I'm sure this is a great job, honey, but instead of a $200 sale, where you made no commission, you could have made $50 to $100 for doing the same great job with us in less than thirty minutes."

"Well, they treat me really great here, and something like what you're talking about, I might not make anything. It's kind of risky, especially with the economy. You just never know what will happen." Allie didn't want to lose her job with the Balls for All Occasions store, or the security it provided.

"I understand, and I thought that way in the beginning as well. As soon as Scott retires next week, my business will be our primary income. I'm Pat McClure, by the way." Holding out her hand, Allie shook it.

"Take my card, and if you decide you want more information, just give me a call when you get off. We can meet for a coffee and I'll tell you how to get started. We Nova Ladies have lots of fun." She winked as she left with her husband, carrying their purchases.

Dismissing it from her mind, Allie left the register to go help more customers.

~~~

Two days later, Allie noticed the business card sticking out from under the register.

"Let's see if this McClure lady knows what she's talking about." Running her sales total from the day, she was surprised to see $1500 in sales. Only making a little more than minimum wage, her pay for the day was about $85.

Allie thought to herself, *Whoa, I could've made closer to $500, or even $800 for working all day. It would be nice to have additional cash flow coming in. Maybe I should give her a call so we can meet tomorrow.* Dialing the number on her phone as she walked to her car, she was startled when it was answered immediately.

"Mrs. McClure? This is Allie from the Balls for All Occasions sports store. Could we meet tomorrow, say about eight a.m. for coffee? I'd like to hear more about becoming a Nova Lady."

~~~

As six weeks passed at her new job, Allie realized being a Nova Lady was her true calling.

Being my own boss is wonderful, she thought as she stopped to make her first delivery of the day at the Curl Up and Dye salon.

"Hey, ladies." Allie sailed in and got right to business. "I've got the new nail polish you wanted to look at. It's called Hot Sprinkles. They come in green, purple, pink, and blue." Loving being able to help ladies build their self-confidence was more fun than working for someone else.

All five ladies, even the customers with rollers in their hair, crowded around to check out the new samples.

"I'll take two sets—one for the shop, and one for my daughters." Britany was the nail tech in the small salon, so she had final say on the purchases for her department.

"Have you got anything on special, Allie?" Jessica, the stylist, was always on the lookout for a bargain.

"I have lipsticks on sale, two for $8.99. Here are the shades it's available in." Allie held out the basket with small samples of each lipstick.

"Oh, this dark brown would look good on you, Jessica. It goes well with your coloring." Britany held one up to Jessica's cheek. "Mary Beth, you have to try this one, darling. It would go great with that dress you got last week, wouldn't it ladies?" Chorusing agreements from the other ladies led to each woman purchasing several lipsticks.

Writing their orders down and giving them their totals, Allie hurried out to her next delivery at Miss Barbara's house.

Miss Barbara was a character, and when she was given a time to expect Allie, there was no being late, or she would call to find out the reason she wasn't there. Not answering wasn't an option, because Miss Barbara would continue calling until the phone was answered.

Arriving five minutes early—*no lecture today*—Allie breathed a sigh of relief.

Taking the $10 order from the back seat and gathering a new brochure, she headed into what she had begun to call 'the inquisition.'

"Hey, Allie. You're very punctual today. That's not a trait most of this younger generation understands. Won't you come in?" Miss Barbara's eighty years were no excuse for using bad manners.

"Thank you, ma'am." Allie was unconsciously adding a southern accent to her words the longer she was in Texas.

"Have a seat." Waving to the flowered couch covered in clear plastic, Miss Barbara sat across from her and pulled out a pack of cigarettes. "Would you like one, dear?"

"No, thank you, but I appreciate the offer."

"Oh, that's right. You don't smoke. Well, old habits and all. Hope you don't mind if I do?" Allie nodded in acceptance, and she lit it up. "They keep telling me it's bad for my health, especially since I have to have oxygen on bad days when the wind starts blowing." She pointed to the oxygen tank placed next to her chair.

She chuckled to herself about the irony; Miss Barbara needing the oxygen to breathe, yet she just couldn't live without her cigarettes. Even if it meant blowing up the oxygen tank were she to get too close to it.

Miss Barbara seemed to always enjoy visiting with Allie, even if she was unable to purchase large amounts of Nova items. It was Allie's job, and the Nova way, to make each customer feel appreciated, even the difficult ones.

Leaving Miss Barbara, she opened the trunk to use the body spray she kept for such purposes to help mask the smell of smoke on her clothes. Allie never really noticed it, but since people weren't smoking as much these days, they were more sensitive to the smell.

The next stop on her list was Dollie's Salon, where one could always expect to hear the latest gossip as soon as it happened.

Today was no exception. The ladies couldn't wait to tell Allie what was going on at the high school.

"Did you hear what happened Friday when school let out?" Allie shook her head no, so Christy continued. "Well, they caught the band teacher, Rod Martin, and the English teacher, Stacy, doing it in the storage closet."

"Wow! They were hooking up in the closet? Who caught them?" Allie asked in disbelief.

Dollie chimed in. "The school administration fired Stacy, but Rod, the band director, still has his job. The board placed some conditions on him for him to keep it. He has to take the band on its trip to Washington D.C. in three weeks. If he wants to go, he and Stacy have to get married so he can be the chaperone for the trip. Can you believe it?"

"Uh, I'm not even sure what to say. How is it possible that Mr. Martin can keep his job, while she loses hers? Isn't that a little sexist?" Allie had no idea how rural this area was in regards to female rights, but she was finding out that just because parts of the country were modern, the small towns were stuck in a time warp.

"It's not fair. Nobody ever said it was, but that's how things are around here. The old guys run the school board, and what they say goes. Mr. Martin's been the band director forever now, and Stacy has only been here a few years, so she's the dispensable one. Mr. Martin wins state competitions so they're willing to keep him at all costs." Dollie gave a helpless shoulder shrug, as if to say, *'What can you do?'*

"On the positive side, we have a wedding to go to. So, what have you got in that basket of yours?"

"I have the new bottle of Sexy Lady. It'll definitely help with the after wedding dance date." Allie passed it around for them to try on.

"Will it be here in time for the wedding?" Christy asked.

"Oh, yes. I'll have it for you by next week. Is that enough time, ladies?" Allie put the bottle back in the basket as she waited for their decision.

"I'll have to call you later, once I see how this smells on my skin. You know some of these perfumes make me smell like skunk pee." Dollie always mentioned this when trying something new.

"Well, it smells wonderful on me, so put me down," Christy announced.

Collecting the other orders from the last brochure, Allie waved goodbye and left amid laughter as the ladies moved on to the next interesting piece of gossip.

Megan's house was next on the list, and by far Allie's favorite, since they would get to visit while eating lunch.

They had met at the Balls for All Occasions sports store when Allie sold Megan cleats for her daughter's first T-ball game and became friends as Megan ordered her makeup over the past few weeks.

Allie hadn't made many friends since moving to Texas, but she hit it off with Megan instantly.

Allie didn't notice anything unusual as she turned the corner, approaching Megan's house. Hopping out of the car to grab Megan's order, she slammed the door shut and turned to walk up to the house.

    Her hand flew to her mouth as she stopped in horror at the sight that greeted her. The door was hanging off the hinges and partially open. It was a pretty good sign of what she could expect to find inside.

Chapter 2

"What the hell is going on?" Allie muttered as she approached.

Pushing the door back into place so she could enter, she called out, "Hello? Megan, are you here?"

Allie gingerly stepped inside and her heart broke. Everywhere she looked, there were signs of a violent struggle.

Cushions were thrown off the couch. The coffee table was bashed in, and there were blood stains on the carpet.

Torn between trying to find Megan alive and needing to call 911, Allie's decision was made for her as a whimper sounded from down the hall.

Stepping carefully around the broken glass and the blood trail leading her down the hallway, she followed the sound, only to discover Megan in the bathroom, sitting on the floor. She was curled up next to the bathtub, holding a towel to what looked to be a nasty wound on her head.

"Oh, Megan. What happened?" Allie crouched down and leaned forward to touch her arm in sympathy, but Megan flinched back, moaning in pain.

"I'm here, Megan," she said quietly. "No one can hurt you now. I'm going to call the police and figure out how to keep you safe."

Megan looked up at Allie and burst into tears.

"Shh. Everything will be okay. We'll find the person who did this to you." Allie tried to look over Megan's body to assess her injuries, needing to know if there were others she had to worry about.

A smile flitted across Megan's face. "You won't have to look far for the person who hurt me. It was Mike. He does this occasionally when I don't do what I'm supposed to."

Allie suddenly realized that her favorite little person was missing. "Megan, is Sally okay?"

"She was already on the bus, heading to school when it started this time." Megan groaned as she tried to sit up.

"Don't move. Have you been in here since then?" She looks down at her watch. "You've been in here for four and a half hours? Jesus. We need to get you to the hospital and call the police." Allie was worried Mike would make another appearance before she could get Megan to a safe place.

Megan's already pale face grew ashen when Allie's words sank in. "No! If Mike comes home and finds me gone, I'll get a lot worse next time for taking this out into the public. It'll reflect badly on his image with his co-workers."

"Megan, honey, we can't worry about his "image." You're hurt, and I'm pretty sure you need stitches on your forehead. You could have a concussion. From the looks of the living room, you may even have internal injuries that we can't see." Allie didn't want to pressure her, but there was no way Megan could stay home and just recover.

"It was my fault this happened," Megan tried to explain. "Mike got drunk last night and fell asleep in his truck. Because I didn't try to find him, he felt humiliated when the neighbors saw him this morning. He was pretty pissed when he woke up and came inside."

"Megan, this is not your fault. Listen, you have to leave now, go to the hospital and get help. If you stay here, the next time I come to see you, you could be lying dead on the floor. What if he hurts Sally?" Allie held her breath, waiting for Megan's answer.

"I don't know where we would go, and Mike works for the County Sheriff's Office. He can find us wherever we go, and it won't be good when he catches up to us." Megan closed her eyes against the pain.

"So, if you stay here and take everything he dishes out to you, what happens when he starts taking it out on Sally because she spills her juice? Even if he never lays a hand on her, it still gives her the idea that it's okay to get bullied and beaten up. Is that what you want her to feel?" Allie sighed, overwhelmed by the idea that anyone could do this much harm to someone they claimed to love.

Sensing Allie's concern, Megan nodded in agreement. Things were only going to get worse if they didn't leave now.

With the small gesture, Megan's head began to pound in pain, increasing from a quiet drum beat to a loud jackhammer, causing her to feel nauseous. Megan's physical condition was the deciding factor she needed to get help.

"We can leave today. I have some suitcases in the front closet that are packed. This has been going on for years now, and I thought this was the end for me this morning. I'm pretty lucky it wasn't."

Moving slowly as she tried to get up, Megan spoke softly. "We just need to get my purse and add a few things from Sally's room she might miss when we're gone."

"Don't worry, I'll gather everything and put it in the car, then I'll come back for you." Allie went to the living room and surveyed the damage Mike had done to his own home.

Because Mike was a sheriff's deputy, it would be much worse for Megan than if he were just an ordinary guy when it came to evidence being misplaced, or simply disappearing.

"I need to document this in case the evidence against him is suddenly lost." Allie pulled out her phone and stepping outside to take pictures of the front door. She worked her way through the room, then followed the trail of blood until she stood in the bathroom doorway, where Megan still sat with her eyes closed.

She wanted to make sure there was no doubt about what had happened.

Allie placed the packed suitcases by the front door, and tried to remember what all she'd needed when she was forced to leave her home as she walked through the house.

Noticing the boxes stacked in the laundry room, Allie grabbed two and began to pack everything she could fit from Sally's and Megan's closets. Four boxes of clothes and shoes later, she went back to check on Megan to make sure she was still conscious.

"What else do you want so you don't have to worry about coming back? Or is there anything you don't want him to destroy that you really love and want to keep?" Allie asked as she paused in the doorway.

"Did you get Sally's baby doll and her blanket? Also, the photo albums in the living room…and my laptop computer on the bedside table would be great. I should really help you with all this." Making a move to rise, Allie caught her and helped her back to the floor.

"Absolutely not. I have it under control. When I get the boxes in the car, we can go. I can handle it. I'm not the one who has a bloody head and a possible concussion."

Heading toward Megan's room for the computer, she looked around to make sure she hadn't missed anything else they might need. As she was grabbing the photo albums and the address books from the desk, Allie remembered Megan might need birth certificates, and a few other important documents in the days ahead.

Sticking her head back into the bathroom, she asked, "Where do you keep yours and Sally's birth certificates and other stuff?"

Megan was caught off guard because she hadn't thought about needing things like that.

"They're in the filing cabinet; the first three files in the drawer should have all the stuff we need in them." She breathed a sigh of relief that it was all together. Megan felt better knowing that her friend could take care of these things for her right now.

"When will Mike be back to check on you? Will he be home for lunch, or after his shift?" Allie was concerned he might return soon.

"It looks like he showered after I passed out in the living room, because the towel was wet when I crawled in here. He must have gone to work after, and he shouldn't be back until his shift is over," Megan answered.

"Okay, I think I have everything. I just need to carry these last few things to the car. I'll make a final sweep, then we can get you out of here."

Allie carried the boxes to the car and took one last look around, and thankfully spotted the DVDs Sally would enjoy to pass the time and keep her occupied while they sorted things out.

Returning for Megan, she realized she'd forgotten the bathroom toiletries. Grabbing a sheet from the cabinet, Allie filled it with all of Megan's personal hygiene products.

She had left the passenger door open for Megan, as she placed the final things in the backseat.

Allie wrapped an arm around Megan's waist to help her off the floor. They stood still for a second so that Megan could gain her balance. After a few minutes, it was obvious to Allie that her friend wasn't going to get better, no matter how long they waited.

Balancing Megan's body weight carefully, Allie practically carried her to the car, hoping she hadn't hurt her worse.

"Are you okay? Am I hurting you?" Allie paused as Megan moaned.

"No. Seeing the door hanging off the hinges, I'm realizing how angry he truly was. I think this is the right choice. It's a good thing Sally was already at school. Who knows how it might have turned out otherwise." Gently helping Megan down the steps to the car, Allie had a revelation.

"Megan, you need to call the school and let them know that I'll be picking Sally up today." Putting Megan's feet in the car, she shut the door as she walked over to the driver's side.

"Where's my phone?" Megan asked, but didn't have the energy left to look for it.

"It was sitting on the table. The screen was shattered, and a hammer was lying right next to it. I took pictures of it and put it in a baggie, just in case we can save the sim card for another phone."

Allie looked up the number for the school and handed her the phone as she started the car.

"Hi, Ms. Judy? This is Megan Butts, and I needed to let you know that Sally will be picked up today by my friend, Allie Foster."

"Is everything okay, dear? You've never had someone pick Sally up before," Ms. Judy asked with concern in her voice.

"Well, I had an accident. I fell and hit my head. I'm okay, but I'll have to get some stitches. I'm sure they'll give me pain killers, and I won't be able to drive." Megan's first impulse was to make up a plausible story so that Mike wouldn't get mad. She needed to make sure others didn't find out that he beat her.

"You just take care of yourself, and I'll send the papers home with Sally so you can add Allie Foster to the list, just in case you don't feel well enough tomorrow as well." Ms. Judy knew more than she let on about the home life of her students' families, but wisely refrained from saying anything.

"Thank you, Ms. Judy. You're so thoughtful, and I really hope to be better tomorrow. But better safe than sorry, right?"

"Yes, ma'am. I'll have Sally ready for her when she gets here. Get some rest. Bye now." Ms. Judy shook her head at the excuses she heard from the victims of abuse. At least Megan had a friend to help her out. Maybe she would survive and not become a statistic.

Relieved that Sally would be taken care of, Megan tried to ignore the situation by closing her eyes, hoping it would all disappear.

Allie pulled away, leaving the front door hanging wide open.

Chapter 3

At the hospital, Allie drove straight to the ER entrance, and before she could park or make it to Megan's door, a team rushed out to meet them.

"How far apart are her contractions?" one of the attendants asked as they helped Megan out, gently placing her into a wheelchair.

"Uh…I think you have the wrong person. She's not pregnant, she has a concussion."

"Oh, well, we'll get her inside and see what her injuries are, but I need you to move so any other emergencies can stop here."

Unsure about leaving Megan in their capable hands, Allie had no choice but to do as they requested, as another car came roaring into the hospital drive.

After parking, Allie made her way inside the hospital. She was glad that Megan was still coherent enough to nod when they asked if she could come back with her. It turned out to be a good thing, since they weren't sure who she was.

"Where is she hurt? Who is she?" They were still trying to get Megan to answer their questions when Allie came into the room.

Megan passed out before she could fill out the forms, and now the nurses were looking for anything that could tell them how to help her. Considering she probably had a concussion, it was a small miracle that Megan had remained conscious for so long.

"What happened? Was she in an accident?"

Answering their questions about what had happened to Megan, she explained to the best of her knowledge the circumstances of her injuries.

"From what she told me, her husband began hitting her until she passed out, leaving her lying unconscious while he went to work." Hoping to protect Megan, Allie had checked the box to restrict who could know she was in the hospital.

"I need to know that you won't call the sheriff's office about this, because he works for them." She wanted to convey the urgency of the situation. "You can't put her information in the system. Her husband will then know she came in to be treated."

"Ma'am, we have to file a police report for this kind of situation, but we can call in the local police instead. I think I can word the report so it won't arouse suspicion if they broadcast it over the radio. Don't worry, we'll take care of her." A few of the nurses began wheeling an unconscious Megan out for X-rays and a CAT scan. "Are you family?"

"No, but I'm the one she wants to pick her daughter up, so temporary guardian, maybe?"

"Well, I can't let you go back with her, but you can wait in the family area. When you fill out the paperwork, there's an emergency contact spot. You might want to make sure you're on the list so when we update the system…well, you get the idea." The nurse winked conspiratorially. "We'll see what the doctor will tell you when he's finished examining her." The nurse patted Allie on the back and pointed her toward the waiting area.

Sitting in the lounge, Allie glanced at the clock. She was surprised to see it was only one o'clock. With everything that had happen, it seemed so much later than it really was. Time had seemed to slow down the moment she had pulled up to Megan's house.

Taking the nurse's advice, Allie finished filling out the paperwork and returned it to the nurse's station.

"Here's the information for Megan Butts. I was wondering if there was a local women's shelter that I could contact about her situation? Also, do you have the number for a good lawyer?"

"Yes. Here's the number for Mark Greenley, and the shelter's number is on the bulletin board over by the snack machines." Sliding a paper with the number on it, she then waved her in the direction of the bulletin board.

"Thank you so much." Allie went to find the information and placed the calls in semi-privacy.

The Umbrella Shelter lady was very helpful as Allie explained the situation to her. "We can send someone over right now to pick them up, but it's better to wait until she files the police report."

"Oh. She isn't able to go anywhere right now. They have her up in X-ray to see how badly hurt she is. We just need some information so she'll know what her options are, and where she can go when she does leave the hospital."

"It sounds like you're a good friend to stick around while they take care of her. I can have someone come over this afternoon, and we can work out what her choices are. She should be safe while she's in the hospital. The staff and security will keep her husband out." Sounding certain about Megan's safety, Allie considered what they needed to do next.

"I have to pick her daughter up from school, but I should be back by four o'clock. I'm sure the police will talk to her before then, so we'll have a clearer picture of the situation. I appreciate your help, and we'll see you then." Allie hung up and proceeded to call the lawyer.

"Hi, Mark Greenley's office. How may I help you?" Startled, Allie had no idea what to tell the receptionist.

"Um, I have a friend who's in the hospital. She's going to need legal counsel regarding custody of her daughter, and possible divorce. Does Mr. Greenley take those types of cases?"

"Yes, ma'am, he does, and I'm guessing it's a fairly urgent situation?" Learning how to tell the difference between urgent and non-urgent was the sign of an efficient secretary.

"It is, and needs to be kept quiet so the father doesn't find out. The mother's in the hospital getting X-rays right now, so is there any way he could come a little later this afternoon? If he could make it by three, it would help a lot." Allie wanted to be available in case Megan needed her to run errands, or interference.

"Yes. I'll send him around three today. Who should he ask for?"

"Megan Butts, or Allie Foster. Thank you so much. I have to go; the police are here." Allie saw the police officers heading toward the nurse's station, and went to give her statement.

In the family waiting room, Allie spent the next hour answering questions.

"Ms. Foster, were you there at the time of the incident?" The short, slightly overweight policeman, Officer Long, asked rather gruffly.

"No. I wasn't there when it occurred, but I got there at about eleven, and I know Sally rides the bus at 7:15. I'm not sure how long she was unconscious before I got there, though. I only saw the aftermath of what happened. I took pictures of the scene before we left, just in case he came back and tried to clean it up." Allie really hoped that they would be able to arrest Mike for what he had done.

"So you didn't see this alleged assault?" Officer Long seemed to doubt it had even occurred.

"No, I wasn't there, but I believe the hospital will confirm that Megan was assaulted." Allie tried to take a calming breath so she didn't lose her temper and hurt the officer herself.

"In other words, we only have your word that her husband, Mike Butts, a highly-commended deputy, did this to her? How do we know it wasn't a random burglary?" He pointed his pen accusingly at Allie, as if to say she had done it.

"All right. I've been polite, sir, but just because you're acquainted with her husband, doesn't mean he didn't do this to her. Just because you don't believe me is no excuse to make accusations and not take my statement. Do I need to call your supervisor so they can take care of this situation? My friend needs to be taken care of, and I want to make sure she's placed in a safe environment, along with her daughter," she stated sternly.

Hearing the last part of Allie's concern, Officer Julie Grayson, who just stepped into the room, intervened.

"Leave her alone, Long. She didn't have anything to do with it and you know it." She came up to stand beside her fellow officer. "I'm the ranking officer here, and I'll make sure we manage not to overlook anything you tell us. Now, can you start from the beginning of why you were there and what transpired, please?"

"Um, sure." Slightly confused at the way things were happening, Allie complied by starting at the beginning, *again*. She tried not to leave anything out as she filled them in from when she pulled up at the house, until the time she had left with Megan.

"I only know that what I saw were signs that a big fight had gone down, and then my friend was lying on her bathroom floor with a head wound."

"So, based on what you saw, and from what the victim told you, her husband was the one that did this to her?" Officer Grayson was trying to cover all the bases.

"Yes, ma'am. When I suggested leaving, she was fearful that he would come find them and try to finish the job. She wanted to stay there, even though her injuries were causing her great pain. When I mentioned her daughter, she realized the example she was setting and allowed me to bring her to the hospital." Allie was thankful the woman officer was taking this seriously, while Officer Long rolled his eyes at the mention of Mike punishing them.

"And where is her daughter now? Is she at school?"

"Yes, and I'm supposed to go and pick her up when school lets out. Will that be a problem?" Allie really didn't want Sally to go back into Mike's custody.

"Of course it will, since you're not related to them, and only have the permission and say of an incoherent woman." Officer Long smiled as he delivered his winning statement.

"Megan called the school and authorized me to pick her up, and the secretary's expecting me. I've also spoken to a lawyer, who's supposed to be here around the time Megan gets back from her examination." Watching the triumphant smile slip from his arrogant face, Allie continued. "I have all the pictures I took of the damage. I'll send them to you, and to my email as well so they don't get misplaced. Oh, and here's her phone. It was smashed on the table. I wasn't sure if we could use the sim card so she would still have her numbers available." Allie turned to open her purse and hand it to them, when Officer Long piped in again.

"This is a police matter, and you shouldn't have touched anything in that home. You should've called us immediately. The crime scene is now contaminated because of what you did, and it won't help your case if you planted evidence to frame a sheriff's deputy." He puffed out his chest to emphasize his statement.

Pointing her finger in Officer Long's face, Allie explained the situation. "Excuse me, but the local police department was called and not the sheriff's office. She was extremely worried her husband, with whom you are acquainted, would find out she was in the hospital before she was somewhere safe. Her well-being and the evidence being misplaced or covered up was something I was *not* going to take a chance on."

Hearing Officer Grayson snicker, Allie gained a little more confidence. "I'm not saying you'll hide anything, but just because he's your fellow officer, I won't be intimidated. Now, where do you want the photos I've taken sent to?" Allie turned her attention to the female officer.

"Here's my card and information. We'll head over to the Butt's house and take a look at the residence, as well as take some pictures of our own. We're not going to call the sheriff's office, and any attempt to do so by those in my department will be charged with aiding and abetting," she announced as she fixed Officer Long with a pointed look of disdain.

"Can we see the pictures?" Officer Grayson held out her hand expectantly.

"Gladly." Allie unlocked the screen and handed it to her.

"Wow. I'm pretty sure Megan didn't do this to herself." She forced Officer Long to take a look. "He left her in bad shape. Just because he's a member of law enforcement, doesn't give him the right to commit violence against his spouse. Our job is to protect those in our community, and I will be speaking to the DA once we've seen the house."

Officer Long wasn't happy about the situation, or the fact that he had to take orders from his superior, who was a woman. Closing his memo book, he nodded his head at Allie and headed for the door.

Waiting until her partner was out of earshot, Officer Grayson turned back to Allie as she followed him toward the door. "If you need anything at all, please call me at this number." She handed Allie another card with her personal cell number written on the back. "Even if I'm off the clock, I'll make sure I respond to your call. As the only female officer on the town's police force, I can assure you there won't be much sympathy for Mrs. Butt's situation. I'm afraid both of you could be in danger if I'm not present to defuse the situation. 'Accidents' happen in stressful circumstances."

"Thank you, Officer Grayson. As soon as she's awake and talking, I'll text you and let you know what the doctors say about her condition." Allie smiled at her, nodding in the direction Officer Long went. "I don't envy you the car ride to their house."

Officer Grayson grinned as she went out to deal with her cranky partner.

Allie checked in with the nurse to see how things were coming along with Megan.

"It'll be another hour or so before we finish the CAT scan, but she's regained consciousness for short amounts of time, so it's looking a little better for her, unless there are some major complications," the nurse on duty informed Allie.

"I'm going to run some errands before picking her daughter up from school. I should return around three, and if anything changes, give me a call at this number." Allie wrote it down on a Post-it note, handing it to the nurse.

"She should be okay for the next hour or so, but it's good to have, just in case." Taking the number from Allie, the nurse attached it to a chart behind the desk.

Thanking her, Allie headed to her car so she could unload it before picking Sally up.

Passing a storage unit on the way to her apartment, she made a spur-of-the-moment decision and stopped to rent a locker.

Paying in cash with a fictional name worked since the lady didn't bother to question Allie. Living in a small town had its advantages when it came to people being trusting and accepting of whatever they were told.

Allie sorted out what they would need for the next few days, and put everything else in the unit.

Glancing at her watch, she hurried to finish so that she would have time to freshen up after all the moving she had done. Not used to being on a strict schedule, she realized she would have to keep a close eye on time for the next few days, or Sally would be late to school.

Normally, Allie kept her schedule full so she didn't have time to think about her past or worry about her future. Her coping mechanism had managed to keep her self-pity from overwhelming her most days over the past two years in witness protection. Watching over Sally the next few days would be more than enough to keep her too busy for a pity party.

~~~

Finding an empty parking spot at the elementary school, she headed into the school's office.

"Hi, I'm Allie. I'm here to pick up Sally Butts. Her mom called to let Judy know it was okay. Are you Judy?" Allie nervously inquired of the nice, in charge looking lady behind the desk.

"Yes, I'm Judy, and her class will be out shortly. I'll need to get a copy of your license on file, then you can have a seat on the bench over there." Taking the needed license to copy, Judy added, "Here are the papers for Megan to fill out so we can add you to the approved pick-up list in the future." Judy smiled at Allie, trying to reassure her. "Children may come in small packages, but they bounce back quickly with lots of energy to spare."

Allie summoned up the courage to promote her business, since Judy seemed so friendly. "Ms. Judy, do you have someone who brings you Nova brochures?"

Allie might as well use the opportunity provided to her while she was here, but she didn't want take someone's territory if they were already supplying them with products.

"We don't, actually, but you could leave some and I'll put them in the break room for you." Judy smiled at her and whispered conspiratorially, "We're always looking for ways to make some of these older ladies more beautiful, if you know what I mean."

Allie laughed. "Thanks. Will five books be enough? Or do you think you'll need more? We don't want any catfights to start over these life-changing brochures," Allie whispered back.

"Perfect. If we need more by next week, I'll let you know," Judy graciously agreed.

Allie hurried out to the car for the brochures. Spotting a hand lotion sample that would work nicely, she decided to give Ms. Judy a gift for being so nice, and giving her a chance to be the school's Nova Lady.

Ms. Judy was pleasantly surprised when Allie returned with her free lotion. Taking the books, she placed them on the desk. "There's her class now."

Allie waited until Sally spotted her and ran over. "Where's Mommy?" She looked around at the crowd of mothers and children pairing up, hoping for a glimpse of her own mother.

"Hi. I'm Sally's teacher, Susan." She smiled before turning back to Sally. "Sally, what's the rule about leaving the line without permission?"

Her green eyes grew wider as she looked between Ms. Susan and Allie. "Why isn't Mommy here?"

"Sally, that's why I'm here to pick you up today. Something came up and your mom wanted to make sure you didn't ride the bus home." Allie didn't want Sally to panic, because this was something out of the norm for her. Allie then turned to Ms. Susan. "I've already signed her out with the office."

"It's okay, Sally. Ms. Judy said your mother called about Allie picking you up. I'll see you tomorrow, all right?" Ms. Susan was watching Sally closely for a reaction.

Sally nodded, placing her hand in Allie's. At least Sally had been around her before, so she didn't feel like a stranger was picking her up.

Walking toward the car, Sally asked the question Allie had been dreading. "What happened to my mom?"

Seeing no point in sugar coating the truth, Allie decided to be straight with her. They were going to the hospital, and she would see how hurt her mother was anyway.

"Sally, your mom was in an accident this morning and she's at the hospital. When I left, they were taking X-rays to see if she had any broken bones." Opening the back to let Sally climb in, she dealt with the next issue about Megan's health. "Your mom will look bruised and bandaged, but she's a good sport. She was worried you would be scared when you saw her, but you're a big girl, and a mummified mommy wouldn't scare you, right?" Allie had no idea how to deal with a child who was upset, so she tried to make light of the situation.

Eyes wide, Sally pulled the seat belt over her and buckled it. "Will she have toilet paper all over her body? I'll recognize her, right?"

"Yeah. When she gets better, maybe she'll let you unroll her all the way to the bathroom so you can reuse the toilet paper. Cool, huh?" Stringing her along with a larger tale, Allie waited to see if Sally knew she was being teased.

Laughing at Allie's antics, Sally turned serious. "Seriously, how badly is my mom hurt?"

Allie bent down inside the door. "I think she's going to stay in the hospital tonight, and maybe tomorrow. She has a cut on her head and a couple broken ribs, so we might have to have a slumber party at my house with pizza and movies. Do you think you can handle that while your mom gets better?"

She shook her head in agreement, then asked, "Miss Allie, did my daddy hurt my mommy?"

"Sweetie, your mommy and daddy got into a fight this morning. Your mommy hit her head, and when it didn't get better, I took her to the hospital so they could make her better."

Allie concentrated on checking to make sure the seat belt was securely fastened.

"I don't know if your daddy was hurt or not, because he went to work. When your mommy gets better, both of you are going to stay at my house until she can take care of you." Allie hoped it was the last question, but her relief was short-lived when Sally spoke again.

"I've seen my daddy hit Mommy sometimes at night when I'm supposed to be in bed. I know he hurts her, because she's always telling him to stop. She cries when she doesn't think I'm looking at her." Seeing the tears on Allie's cheeks, Sally wiped them away. "Will they arrest my daddy? Will he go to jail? He's a policeman and locks people up, so who's going to lock him up?" Sally asked innocently.

Allie felt so bad for both of them. Megan thought her daughter hadn't witnessed Mike's abuse, but shielding Sally didn't save either of them emotionally.

"Sally, we can't be sure your daddy will be arrested. The judges and other police officers will have to make sure what happened to determine the kind of punishment he should get. If he goes to jail, then the other officers will have to lock him up." Allie moved to get in the front seat and looked at Sally in the rearview mirror.

"Miss Allie, I don't want my daddy to go to jail with all those bad guys. I love him, but I don't want him to hit on my mommy anymore. It's not nice to hit, and he should have a time out to think about what he did wrong. That's what my teachers say when someone hits other people in our class; they need a time out for bad behavior." Hiding a smile, Allie completely agreed with Sally.

Pulling into the hospital parking lot, Allie tried to reassure Sally. "We're going to concentrate on getting your mommy well and leave your daddy up to the police officers to decide what to do about him, okay?" She watched as Sally nodded in agreement and continued. "You can even make your mom a get well card, so when you're at my house tonight, she'll know you're thinking of her. It'll make her get better faster."

Arriving seemed to slow the tide of questions from Sally as they approached the front doors. Unsure if she could handle two days of questions from the first grader, Allie hoped she could survive.

Driving to the hospital, they were each lost in their own thoughts as they hoped for good news about Megan's injuries.

Chapter 4

They had put Megan into a room by herself so they could monitor who was going in and out. Asking at the nurse's station where her room was, Allie was directed there without any problems since they'd seen her with Megan earlier.

When Sally saw her mother, she started to run, only to slide to a sudden stop at the sight of the IVs and monitors hooked up to Megan.

She looked back at Allie. "Will I break her if I give her a hug?" Allie could see Megan suppressing a chuckle, which turned into a grimace of pain.

"Of course not, honey. You just need to be very gentle. Go ahead and give her a hug and a kiss." Seeing Megan's face break into a smile at seeing Sally, it gave Allie hope that they would make it through this difficult time, as long as they were together.

"Mommy, are you okay?" Sally asked, patting Megan's hand gently. There were twenty stitches across Megan's forehead, and her left arm was wrapped up in a sling. She didn't look wonderful, but at least she was conscious and alive.

Remembering not to shake her head in response to Sally's question, Megan answered cautiously. "Yes, sweetie, I'll be okay. Mommy got hurt, but the doctors have been working on me, and they think I can go home in a few days. Can you stay with Miss Allie until I get better?"

"Sure, Mommy. We talked about it on the way over, and when you're able to leave, you get to come and hang out at Miss Allie's house until you're totally better." Satisfied, since her mother's recovery had been assured, Sally switched gears. "Can I go work on the pictures you told me I could make for Mommy to make her feel better, Miss Allie?"

"Yeah. Let's get you all setup." Opening the bag the nurse had given them at the nurse's station, Allie pulled out the remote control.

As she turned on the TV, Sally chirped, "Put it on the cartoon channel. My favorite comes on after school lets out." Allie hoped the TV would distract her enough to cover any conversation that she didn't need to hear as she pulled the curtain around the empty area where the other bed normally went.

"So, did the doctor agree that you have a concussion?" Allie spoke quietly as she scooted the chair next to the bed.

"He said it was a good thing you got me here when you did, because I'd lost a lot of blood, and during the X-ray, they found my shoulder had been dislocated. They think it's best to keep me here to assess any effects from the head wound. But with all the medication they've given me, I'm not really feeling anything. I'm glad I got to see Sally and let her know everything will be fine."

"I was able to talk to the officers about everything, and I think at least one of them will be helpful. They may show up to speak to you, as well as the lawyer." Allie didn't really want to see Officer Long ever again.

"Lawyer? Why do I need one of those?" Megan was unsure if the pain meds were causing her confusion, or just her concussion.

"Megan, there's nothing to legally stop Mike from showing up at my house or school and taking Sally from you. Also, if you're going to press charges, you're going to need a protective order and a lawyer who's on your side before Mike has any idea what you're doing."

"Oh. I guess I didn't think this through very well. Thanks for looking out for me."

Hearing a knock at the door, Allie didn't even have a chance to stand up before and the officers entered the room.

Seeing the officers enter with a woman Allie didn't recognize, she instinctively went to stand near Sally.

"Hi. We're back, and we need to take your statement, Mrs. Butts. This is Ms. Cooke, a social worker, and she's willing to take Sally to get a snack, if that's all right with the both of you?" Apparently, Officer Long had surveyed the damage to Megan's home from her attack, as he spoke more hesitantly now.

Looking to see what Officer Grayson's opinion was, Allie spoke to Sally when she nodded. "Sally, this lady would like to take you to get a snack while we talk to the police officers."

Hopping up, Sally walked around the curtain to look at the officers. "I know you need to take my daddy to jail for what he did, but be gentle with him, okay?"

Sally appraised the woman standing in front of her. Passing her inspection, she went to wait by the door. "You've got snacks?"

"Here's some cash." Allie pulled some ones out of her pocket, but stopped when Ms. Cook spoke.

"I've got it. We'll give you about thirty minutes. We may go see if there are any new babies in the nursery while we're out as well." Seeing Sally's eyes fill with excitement, Allie hoped this was a safe decision.

As the door shut, Officer Long moved closer to Megan's side. "We really need to get this taken care of, ma'am. What happened exactly?" His tone reflected that he believed this case was a waste of time, but it had to be done.

"I'll tell you what happened, but there's no need to get huffy." Megan scooted up in the bed so she didn't feel as helpless with him standing over her. "Mike, my husband, went to hang out with the guys last night, and I guess he had too much to drink. It was after two in the morning when I dozed off, and he still hadn't made it home. I'm assuming he passed out in the truck after he parked it in the driveway, because when I woke up to get Sally ready for school, it was sitting in its spot in the driveway."

Taking a deep breath, Megan continued. "I'm not really sure what woke him up. It was probably when the school bus honked for Sally. He blames me for not getting him into the house this morning before the neighbors could see him."

Megan hadn't heard the door open, but the man who walked in must have been the lawyer since he was wearing a suit and tie. Motioning Allie to remain silent, he listened from behind the curtain as Megan's story unfolded.

"Anyway, his neck must have gotten a crick in it from where he passed out in the truck. I'd locked the door after Sally left, and he didn't have his keys with him. So he busted in the door instead of waiting for me to unlock it. He came after me and started punching me in the stomach, since that's where the bruises can't be seen.

"Normally, I just take it so he'll get it over with, but this morning, there was no way he was going to cool down. I could see the fire in his eyes and knew if I didn't move out of his way, he would kill me." Seeing she had everyone's attention, Megan tried to finish while keeping her voice from shaking.

"I started to run and he tackled me from behind. Then, I tried to move away and was crawling on my stomach to get out from under his reach. I thought with him landing on the floor with me, he wouldn't be able to recover as quickly. I could smell the alcohol on his breath. I thought if I could scoot away, I could try running for the front door, but he didn't let that happen.

"Moving much faster than I ever imagined he could, he grabbed my ankle and jerked me back toward him. I fell and hit my head on the edge of the coffee table. He pulled me up so hard by my left arm, he dislocated it."

"Is that your assessment or the doctor's?" Officer Long interjected sarcastically.

"The doctor's, which is why my arm is in this sling. They had to pop it back into place. Would you like me to continue, or are there any other questions you need to ask?" Megan matched the responding to the officer's accusatory tone with one of her own.

"I was facing him on my knees, trying not to pass out when he placed both hands on my waist and shoved me backward on top of the coffee table, making it collapse. Once I was on my back, he started hitting me again, mostly in the ribs and stomach. I was hurting in so many places, I didn't have a chance to protect myself, not that it would have helped. I think I passed out after a while, and it must have taken the fun out of it for him because he was gone when I came to. I crawled to the bathroom because I was afraid if I tried to stand up, I would pass out again."

Prepared for the officer's next comments, Megan finished her statement. "I didn't want to call the police. It wouldn't have helped since he's one of you. I was just going to rest and clean up before Sally got home, but I must have passed out again because it was several hours before I woke up again, and Allie had arrived for lunch.

"When Allie offered to bring me to the hospital, I wasn't going to let her, but as I tried to get up, I realized I was hurt much worse than I thought. Now that I've come here for help, there's no way I can go back home. He'll make me pay for reporting it, and this time, I can't ignore what he's done. Sally shouldn't have to see this kind of thing happen to her mommy." Exhausted from reliving everything, Megan fell back against the pillows, ready to get some sleep, but knew it would be impossible until she had satisfied Officer Long's suspicions.

"I just hate we have to report this. What if he just apologizes? You could go back home then, right?" Officer Long was hoping they could ignore pressing charges and take care of the incident quietly and off of the books.

About to make his presence known to the officer, Mark, the lawyer, was saved when Officer Grayson took over.

"From what Megan just told us, and what we saw at the crime scene, we have a pretty good idea of what happened. And no, Long, an apology won't work. We have to process this like the attacker was a total stranger to us. Geeze, Long, I'm going to recommend that you go back through sensitivity training after this is all over."

Moving to block Megan's view of her partner, she continued. "You were assaulted, ma'am, and that will come with consequences for your husband. We take these kinds of things very seriously so it won't happen again. Since Mike is a deputy, he knows the legal ramifications of what he's done. Apparently, he never expected you to follow through on your end."

Officer Grayson explained the next part of the process. "We'll file a report with our boss, and the DA will hopefully charge Mike and hold him without bail, but since he has connections, he'll probably get out. If not tonight, then by tomorrow. If you can get a lawyer who can see a judge about a protective order, that will help us immensely."

The man in the suit stepped out from behind the curtain. "No need to inform a lawyer. I've been listening to the whole story. I'll file the paperwork and have her sign a temporary custody order for Allie here so Mike can't make any waves about Sally."

Mark made it a point to stand as far away from Officer Long as possible.

"I'll check in with you in the morning to see how you're doing," Officer Grayson assured. "Just get some rest, and we'll do our best for you. I've already alerted the nurses not to let your husband in, and to call security if he's seen hanging around." She motioned for Officer Long to proceed her from the room, concerned he might do something dumb before she could get him to the parking lot and away from the victim.

~~~

"Hi, I'm Mark Greenley. I'll most definitely take your case." He smiled at Megan and Allie. "I'll file a motion with the court for extreme circumstances, and we shouldn't have any problems getting Allie appointed as a temporary guardian for Sally until you get out of the hospital. Do you want her to have medical authority to make decisions if worst case happens to you? Someone needs to be able to make those decisions, and since she has Sally, it would be a good idea for her to be able to do that as well."

Mark paused, waiting for Megan's answer, hating that he felt the need to push the worst-case scenario possible.

"Yeah, I'm okay with that. But what kind of papers do I need to fill out? I'm just ready to be done with all of this." Megan could feel the pain meds wearing off, and they were the only thing buffering the people she had to deal with from letting her anger out.

"Just these three papers; protective order, custody, and medical. I need your signature at the bottom. We'll have them typed up at the office and you'll be good to go." Mark had already called the judge's chambers before going to the hospital in order to expedite the processing of the protection orders. "I'll run these over to the judge. I can come back in the morning to discuss a course of action, and see if you want to proceed with a divorce."

"How will I pay you? I don't have any money with me. Mike is in charge of all our finances." Megan tried to get up to find her purse.

"Don't worry about it. We can discuss that tomorrow as well. I won't let money come between having you and your daughter protected from harm. Do either of you know what a protective order does?" Both ladies shook their heads no, so Mark explained. "It's so that the father cannot have custody or come within 500 feet of where either you or Sally are residing. Since he's in law enforcement, this will make things more difficult to enforce, but we'll recommend to his supervisor over at the sheriff's office that he be removed from duty and placed on leave until this is resolved. Also, as part of the order, he'll have to turn his gun in, since we have reason to believe he's considered high risk, and is very likely to commit violence not only against himself, but to others as well.

"The judge has scheduled an emergency hearing for me to get this taken care of on Megan's behalf. You have your friend, Officer Grayson, to thank for that. She's really gone to bat for you.

"I can guarantee that your husband has been informed of every detail of this incident, and is aware of where you and Sally are at the moment." Marked turned his attention to Allie. "For tonight, I would advise you to take Sally to your house, but report anything that seems out of place or suspicious to you. I have your information, and if there's anything that needs to be changed, I'll let you know."

Mark handed Allie his card and turned back to Megan. "Mrs. Butts, we'll do everything we can to make sure your husband is not able to hurt you anymore."

"Thank you, Mr. Greenley." Megan held out her right hand. "We'll see you in the morning."

"Can you bring Sally in to say good night? I'm going to ask the nurse to give me something to help me sleep," Megan asked as exhaustion started to take her over.

Allie followed Mr. Greenley out. "We really appreciate this. It's a relief to know someone's looking out for her."

Mark gave a curt nod. "Not a problem. You have a good day."

As he disappeared, she found Sally and Ms. Cook in the family waiting area, eating a snack.

"Hey, munchkin. Your mom's tired and about to go to sleep, so we need to say good night." Allie waited before speaking to Ms. Cook until Sally was back in Megan's room.

"Thank you so much for looking out for her while we talked to the police. When Megan's ready to take the next step, we'll give you a call to keep you informed of where she'll be staying."

"No problem. Just glad I could help out for a bit. I'll be in the courtroom with the judge and let him know we have a safe place for Sally for now. I look forward to working on this with you to keep Sally safe. Bye, Ms. Foster."

Allie stuck her head in the room, just as Sally finished saying good night to Megan. While they were waiting for the nurse to administer the pain meds, Sally began to gather up her stuff.

"Megan, I'll be back in the morning. I think Sally and I have an evening planned with pizza and movies." Seeing Sally's face light up at the mention of dinner and a movie, Allie grinned. "There were a lot of movies at your house that I haven't ever seen, Sally."

Sally grabbed Allie's hand and started dragging her to the door. "Come on. We need to educate you, missy."

Laughing as she was pulled to the door, Allie blew Megan a kiss as she left the room. "Rest up. We need you healthy."

Relieved that Sally was in good hands, Megan closed her eyes, exhausted from the day's events.

~~~

Sally grabbed Allie's hand as they walked down the hall leading to the parking lot, and began to list what she wanted on her pizza.

"We need to have ham, with lots of cheese and pineapples, but none of those little fishy things or mushrooms. Oh, and can we start the movie while we wait for the pizza guy to come?"

Allie nodded in agreement, which seemed to be the only answer Sally was expecting. At least with Sally, there was no doubt as to what she was thinking. She just blurted out what she wanted and what she was thinking without worrying about how it sounded. Some children were blessed with the ability to be positive, no matter what situation they were placed in.

After a quiet evening of pizza, and what turned out to be two princess movies, Sally finally fell asleep on the couch.

Climbing into her own bed, Allie was relieved she didn't have to work at her other job as bartender that night and could rest. The long day had taken a toll on her, leaving her worn out.

~~~

Seven a.m. came much earlier than Allie was used to, being up and coherent. Her new Nova job allowed for a flexible schedule, and with her late nights at the bar, early morning hours was not a time of day that Allie saw often.

Allie's sympathy grew for the parents who had to wake up early every day to get their children ready for school. Sally knew the routine and helped to get things ready so Allie could get her to school on time.

"I'm dressed, Miss Allie. What are we having for breakfast?"

Allie groaned, not having thought that far ahead. As she quickly recovered, she announced, "We're going to pick up donuts on the way to school."

Smiling at Sally's excited gasp, Allie waved a finger in her face. "Don't count on this every morning, missy. I'll go shopping later on today, so we can have a healthy breakfast tomorrow morning. Grab your backpack and let's get in the car." Turning to lock the door behind her, Allie hurried to make sure they made it to school on time.

Making a note to add a booster seat to the grocery list, Allie buckled Sally in. "I'll be there to pick you up when school lets out, okay?"

Sally nodded, unworried about that far into the day.

Twenty minutes later, Allie parked at the school and walked Sally in so she could turn in the papers allowing her to pick Sally up.

Kissing Sally on the head as she ran toward the other children who were lining up, Allie felt a pang of loneliness when she realized what was missing from her life. She had no one who depended on her to take care of them.

Trying to fill the empty hole in her life, Allie's Nova business took up a large amount of her time. Becoming involved with growing a team and helping make their lives better had pushed the loneliness back for a short time.

~~~

Allie was tempted to return home and get some rest, but she had missed the rest of her deliveries from the day before, and they needed to be taken care of.

As she left the school and headed to the hospital to see Megan, she realized she needed to hurry so that she could finish her interrupted day and still be done before Sally was out of school.

Megan looked much worse than she had the day before, because the bruises were starting to show up in a colorful array of blues and purples all over her face and arms.

Already awake and sitting up in bed, Megan was enjoying her liquid breakfast as she waited for the doctor to make his rounds and clear her to eat solid food.

"Hey. How did the night go? Did you get Sally to school okay?" Megan was happy to see a familiar face that had no intention of poking another needle into her already pain-filled body.

"We were fine. Although, I had to feed her donuts for breakfast because I didn't have anything ready to eat this morning. I figured it wouldn't hurt her for one day, right?" Allie asked as she pulled a chair up next to the bed.

"I'm sure she was over the moon and will try to get you to do it every morning." Grimacing at the horrible taste of the broth, Megan placed it back on the tray.

"So the lawyer should be here around eleven this morning so I can sign more paperwork. Am I crazy? He wants me to file for a divorce from Mike." Megan sounded uncertain about the lawyer's intentions.

"It should help with keeping custody of Sally, and making sure Mike won't be able to harm you or her in the future."

"I'm just not sure I'm ready to divorce him. I mean, if I hadn't made him so mad in the first place, none of this would have happened. So it's really not his fault. I should just let him apologize, right? Then we can move on and forget this ever happened."

Megan had spent the night wondering how she would be able to make it on her own. She knew she didn't have any skills she could use to join the workforce. She wouldn't be able to provide a stable home for Sally, and Mike wouldn't let them go without a fight.

"Megan, this has to be your decision. I can't force you to leave Mike or divorce him. You have to want a better life for you and Sally. If you think your future is with him, then call him right now and tell him that. If you don't want to call Mike or go back to him, you have to be prepared. Things may get worse before they get better. I'll support you, but you need to know what path you want to take so you can prepare yourself and follow it." Allie waited, hoping her words would sink in. She didn't want to sugarcoat the consequences of her choices. Neither one would be an easy path to follow.

"I'm going to go and finish my deliveries, but I'll be back some time after ten. In the meantime, you need to figure out what you're going to do so you can tell the lawyer when he gets here." Standing up, Allie reached over and patted Megan's hand. "I'm rooting for you. I'll see you later."

Allie went to the closest bank because she needed to deposit the money from yesterday. She wasn't comfortable with having cash on her. Living in a big city for most of her life, it had made her cautious about safety.

She unloading the box full of orders for the ladies at the bank, and collecting the demo of her newest fragrance from the trunk, she armed herself with the latest brochures, ready to sell makeup.

Allie had set a goal to sell at least ten bottles of perfume this week by giving a ten-dollar discount as an incentive. She would still make five dollars a bottle, improving her sales level and keeping her on track for her year-end goals.

By giving the ladies a discount, it allowed them to save money and created customer loyalty through great customer service.

The fun part of her job was delivering orders to women from all different walks of life. This allowed Allie a chance to feel involved in their lives when they chatted about their daily activities.

Bracing herself with a smile, she started with a story to cheer others up and make them laugh whenever possible.

"So today's story is about a little girl of about two. She was playing with empty pots and pans on her mom's floor. When her mommy walked in, she casually asked her daughter, "What are you cooking?" The little girl looked up at her and replied, "The children." Her mother was horrified as the little girl's words sunk in. "What do you mean, you're cooking the children?" Rolling her eyes, the little girl answered, "Mommy, I'm cooking Hansel and Gretel." Needless to say, this mother would be very careful which fairytales she read to her daughter in the future." Enjoying a good laugh with the ladies was just what Allie needed to shake off her gloomy mood.

"So who has hairy warts that we need to hide with some foundation and concealer?" Allie directed the conversation back to the topic of their orders.

It was early, and there weren't any customers in the bank so the ladies were free to shop without neglecting their jobs or duties.

The box emptied quickly as each lady claimed her order and placed one for the next week.

Allie took care of her deposit and walked out of the building. After selling two more perfumes, she had gained four new orders. Planning on a lighter schedule this next week due to Megan's situation, it was nice to take advantage of a Nova Lady's flexible schedule. Being the boss came with its own advantages.

~~~

Managing to get everything from yesterday taken care of, Allie made a mental to-do list as she drove back to the hospital. After meeting with the lawyer, she would run to the store to get Sally some healthy food to munch on and a car seat. Then, she would call and ask her boss at the bar for a few days off, at least until Friday night, when he would need her the most.

The doctor was in the room when Allie walked in.

"As I was saying," he paused, acknowledging Allie's entrance. "I believe that with rest, spending one more night in the hospital for observation would be for the best. I would be willing to send you home tomorrow if everything still looks good. Do you have a place to go and rest without overdoing it?" He glanced at Allie to see her response to his news of Megan's departure.

"She and her daughter will stay with me until she's up and ready to rock and roll again." Allie made the offer, although she wasn't sure anyone would get much rest until the situation with Mike was resolved.

"Did you hear that, Allie? Only one more night and I can hang out with you and Sally," Megan exclaimed excitedly before turning back to the doctor. "So my concussion is gone, and I can leave, right?" Megan was hopeful about a hospital discharge, even though it made her nervous to be unprotected.

"Yes. You may experience some headaches over the next week, but unless it becomes a full-blown migraine, just take some Advil until you feel better. I'll check back in on you before I leave for the day."

Megan waited until the doctor was gone before asking the question troubling her the most. "I know you were frustrated earlier when I mentioned going back to Mike, but I just don't know anything else. I don't know how to survive on my own. So, if you were serious about letting us crash at your place until I get back on my feet, we'll take you up on it." Megan looked so vulnerable as she put her decision out there with hope in her eyes.

Not wanting to be overly excited for fear of scaring her away, Allie responded with certainty. "Absolutely. Who else can take care of you better than Sally and I?"

Allie thought back to when she had first come to Texas, and those lonely days in WITSEC. She wouldn't wish that on anyone. "Duh. Watching movies with you will be the best."

Smiling, Megan hurried to assure Allie. "It'll only be for a few days, until I can move around better. The ladies from the Umbrella Shelter stopped by this morning and told me about halfway house, so I can get on my feet before we move out on our own."

"Well I'll keep you as long as you'll let me. I need to get better acquainted with all these princesses. Sally informed me about of my lack of education last night." Allie was glad she could put a smile on Megan's face.

Megan had only managed to gain a vague idea of what Allie's younger years were like, but couldn't imagine not knowing who the princesses were. She was glad they could help fill Allie's home with fun and laughter.

"Thanks for being willing to take such good care of us when you really didn't have to."

Allie just nodded at Megan, and the two sat in silence for a while. They were thankful Mr. Greenley interrupted their painful family memories when he walked into the room.

"Hello, ladies. Mrs. Butts, you're looking much better, and more coherent today. Did the nurses take good care of you last night?" Mark flashed Megan a mega-white smile.

Allie didn't hear Megan's response because his smile was so blindingly white. *Geeze, how many times a day does this guy use teeth whitening stuff to get them to look like that? His mouth practically glows. He seems oblivious to the fact his smile is overwhelming,* she thought to herself. Shaking her head to clear the hypnotic cobwebs out, she focused on what Mr. Greenley was saying to Megan.

"Mrs. Butts, they've issued a warrant for your husband's arrest, which they tried to serve yesterday evening around eight. They had to wait and call in the troopers to make sure they had enough manpower to cover it. He didn't resist, but it looks like he's getting out at some point this afternoon if he can make bail." Mr. Greenley felt terrible that he wasn't able to keep him in jail longer.

"He's getting out today? Does he know where I am?" Megan's voice was filled with terror at the thought of Mike finding her.

"I'm certain he'll get a judge who's sympathetic because of his ties to the community as a deputy. They'll release him on his own recognizance. He might not have to post bail to get out of jail. If this was just an assault charge, they wouldn't have issued a warrant for his arrest, but because of your injuries, and the fact it could have resulted in your death, they're charging him with attempted murder."

"Oh, my god. He's going to be so mad that he had to spend the night in jail. I don't think having a protective order will keep him away from me or Sally. If he takes Sally, he knows I'll do anything to make sure that she's safe." Megan began rubbing her hands together in a nervous gesture.

"If he has her, he can make me come home." Megan's machines started to beep as her heart rate increased.

Focusing his attention solely on Megan, Mr. Greenley explained what they could do to help the situation.

"If we file for divorce today, we can seek an immediate relief to stop all the accounts until the judge can fairly divide the assets. Do you have any money or assets outside of your shared bank account?"

"Mike has control of the bank and savings accounts. I have withdrawal slips and a debit card, but I have no idea what's in the accounts." Megan wasn't certain that they even had any assets.

"Since you were forced to leave for fear of your physical safety, and have no outside monetary support, I'm going to request a copy of the bank statements. The judge should be willing to allow you up to $500 for living funds until a final decision is made. Until this investigation is over and you have child support, there's not a lot of options available to you."

Terrified, Megan squeaked out, "You have no idea what he'll do if I take that much money out of our account. I'm only allowed money for the groceries, unless he tells me something else to buy for the family. I even have to give him the receipts so he can use them for the accounting program. Oh, this is so not good."

"Megan." Allie walked over to her and took her hand. "Sweetie, you won't have to answer to him again. The judge will be standing between you and Mike, and making sure that Mike does what he's supposed to do. Mike can't fault you for what the judge decides. The state collects child support, and if he doesn't pay, the judge can have him arrested. Plus, we can get you in some housing and food programs, so you don't have to worry until this divorce is final and earning your own money. Right?" Allie looked to Mr. Greenley for affirmation.

"Yes, since you're the victim, and there's a chance he could make life difficult with his connections. Normally, you would have to stay in the same county, but we're going to explain the situation so you may take Sally somewhere for safety reasons. They'll just ask that I know your whereabouts, and you'll have to stay in the state. These special circumstances will make it more difficult to find you, but not impossible, since Mike can still ask his pals to be on the lookout for you.

"The judge did permit the papers for temporary custody. Or, in case of your death, Sally would remain in Ms. Foster's care until they could investigate the case. Nothing will be permanent until the charges are determined and it's decided that he's a continuing threat to yours and your daughter's safety."

Megan realized she would have to take a leap of faith and press charges against Mike. "So how do I get the divorce started?" She laughed softly. "If I don't do it now and go back to him, then I might as well just kill myself, because that's what he'll do to me." Megan might not understand everything about court procedure, but she knew she needed to protect Sally any way she could.

"We'll have all the paperwork ready to file before he goes in front of the judge this afternoon. The paperwork should be processed before he actually goes to trial. Filing for divorce will provide some extra protection, just in case he tries to get back at you." Mr. Greenley seemed certain as he handed Megan the documents for her signature.

"Here are the papers stating that you're willing to take care of Sally until her mother is able to assume those responsibilities again." Mark handed Allie her own set of papers to sign.

They both signed the papers quickly, then handed them back to Mr. Greenley. Allie hoped they were trusting the right man to keep Megan and Sally safe. Anyone whose teeth were that shiny had to be trying to pull something over on them.

"Thank you, ladies. It has truly been a pleasure. I'll come by in the morning and make sure everything is going okay."

His business demeanor never wavered as he shook their hands and left with the signed papers.

Both ladies' eyes followed him out the door, and Allie was the first to regain her voice. "Girl, he is hot, and he's being very attentive to you. He's working hard to make sure you're well-protected. I don't think most women have this much protection and help when they leave their abusive husbands. I know Mike is a serious threat, but he does seem to be going above the call of duty."

Megan looked flustered. "I'm not sure I'll be ready for a new man anytime soon. I'm so used to having a man who controls everything. Mr. Greenley is cute, but he's taking care of us, just as he would any other client. I wouldn't read anything into it. I just hope he can handle what Mike will try to dish out." She was certain Mike would fight to keep them. She just hoped Mr. Greenley didn't get caught in the crossfire.

"Hey, I wasn't rushing you. I didn't expect you to jump his bones. We were simply appreciating what good *ass*ets the man has." Allie winked at Megan to let her know it was okay to still have a sense of humor.

"I've got to go and get a car seat and swing by work before I pick Sally up. I'll bring her by when she gets out of school and we can hang out for a bit before we go get something to eat. Is that okay with you?"

"Sure. I trust you to take care of her. I'd forgotten about not having a car seat, so thanks for taking care of that as well. I don't know what I would do without you." Megan tried to smile, only to lean back, feeling exhausted again.

"Can you let the nurse know I'll take one of those good pills now, so that I'll be feeling better when Sally gets here?"

"Yes, ma'am." Allie saluted and left to inform the nurse on her way out.

Chapter 5

When Allie picked Sally up from school, she was anxious to see her mom. The two had never really been apart, so this whole situation was trying for both Megan and Sally.

They were only there until Megan's food was delivered, which they left her to eat in peace.

Sally was in a hurry to watch more princess movies and see what Allie was picking up for dinner.

"How does McDonald's sound? Then we can take it to my house and start with whatever movie you think I should watch next." Ruffling Sally's hair, Allie smiled at her enthusiasm.

"Yeah, I love the fries at McDonald's. Oh, I have some homework to do too. It won't take me long, I promise."

After picking up dinner and playing along with Sally's pop quiz about princesses, Allie pulled into her parking lot. She felt the hair on the back of her neck stand up.

"Let's hurry inside, okay? Grab your backpack and I'll grab dinner." Looking around to find the source of her discomfort, she didn't see anyone that stood out.

Locking the door once they were both inside, they spread out on the dining room table.

Still uneasy, Allie walked over to the windows and started closing the blinds.

"The sun sure is bright when those blinds are open. Now we can eat without getting a sunburn." Hearing Sally giggle at her made Allie relax a little.

"Sunburns can come on you in the blink of eye." Snapping her fingers, Allie tried to sound scary. "You never know where a sunburn might be lurking." She wiggled her eyebrows in exaggeration.

"You're silly, Miss Allie. I like hanging out with you," Sally said as she stuffed more fries into her mouth.

"Hey, slow down there, kiddo. The fries aren't trying to escape the deadly sunrays. You can take your time." Keeping the mood light through dinner wasn't hard with Sally's imagination.

"Can you start your homework while I clean up and get things ready for your shower?" Allie asked.

"Ugh! A shower. I took one last night." Sally made a disgusted face.

"No, you didn't. I was here, remember? I would know." Allie shook a finger at her. "See? You thought you could slip something past me, but that won't work, missy. I'm on to you."

"Awe, you're too smart. Sometimes Mom forgets." A sad look flitted across Sally's face.

"Hey, kiddo. If you take a shower and put your jammies on, we can have some popcorn while we watch the movie. Only if you hurry, though."

"Okay. My homework's as good as done."

Allie threw the trash away and went to dig through Sally's suitcase for clothes. Putting everything in the bathroom, Allie hoped Sally was old enough to shower on her own.

Ten minutes later, Sally announced, "I'm done. Let's do this." Sally grimaced, slowly dragging her feet in the direction of the bathroom. It was like she was headed to her doom instead of the shower.

When Allie started to follow her into the bathroom, Sally put her hand up to stop her. "I've got this. After all, I am seven years old. I think I can take a shower by myself."

"Yes, ma'am. I was just going to start the water so it didn't get too hot for you." Allie made a move to leave.

"Well, if you want to for your own peace of mind, I guess that would be all right." Crossing her arms, Sally tried to act casual.

"Just for my peace of mind, then." Barely holding the laughter back, Allie turned the water on and left Sally to her own bath rituals.

While Sally washed up, Allie picked out a movie and started popping the popcorn. Turning to take the popcorn and drinks into the living room, a small figure stepped out from behind the counter, startling her.

"Oh my goodness! Sally, you scared me. Here, take the popcorn so I don't spill it."

"Sure. What are we watching?" Sally questioned.

"Um, I think it has a girl and a frog?" Allie was uncertain about the details, only knowing it was in Sally's stack of favorite movies.

As they settled in together on the couch, Allie was entranced by the music and the story, not once realizing her audience was already asleep until the movie was over.

She covered Sally up and turned the volume down before making her escape to finish her work day.

An order had been delivered that morning, and she had simply set the package inside her apartment until she could get home and sort it into bags for delivery.

Allie placed the bagged orders back into the boxes and carefully stacked them near the front door. A shadow crossed quickly in front of her window, causing her to peer out cautiously.

The person had ducked out of sight, so Allie went to look out the kitchen window, making sure the windows were locked. Only seeing a man walking toward his car, it was hard to tell who it was with the darkening shadows. Since the person was leaving, Allie figured there was no point in calling the police.

Just to be extra cautious, though, she went ahead and locked the deadbolt and chain on the front door, adding a chair under the knob.

Gathering her shoes, keys, and wallet, along with extra clothes for Sally, she put them in her backpack. If something happened, they would be able to make a quick escape.

Hoping these extra security precautions would be enough, she went back to the dining room to finish her work. She had just finished when she heard noise at the front door.

Quickly getting up, she looked out the peephole and saw Sally's dad, Mike, standing just outside.

Wondering how he had found out where Sally was staying, Allie waited to see what he was going to do before calling the police.

She didn't want to cry wolf if nothing happened. If he was only on the premises and didn't do anything, the police might think she was simply making it up because he could leave before they made it to her apartment.

He stood for a minute at the door, then took his hand off the knob and turned, heading toward the parking lot. As he walked, he kept looking back at the apartment, but didn't stop until he got inside a car.

Relieved, she sank to the floor, glad she hadn't called the police. It seemed like he was taunting her, waiting for her to do something.

Allie carried a sleeping Sally to her room and laid her on the bed. She hoped Mike wasn't coming back, but to be on the safe side, she pushed the chest, which had rollers, in front of the back door.

Turning everything off in the living room, Allie grabbed the packed bag and placed it next to her bed. Using the bathroom one last time before she closed the door to her bedroom, she placed a chair under that doorknob as well. She didn't think to wonder where Mike might have gone until the next day.

Chapter 6

Megan was taking medication only when necessary, or after everyone left so she could get some rest. She figured the more rest she got, the sooner she could get out of the hospital. She was sleeping when she felt someone standing over her.

Most of the time, when the nurses entered her room, they would move around and make noise, but this person was just standing over her, quietly, and completely still.

Megan began to feel uncomfortable, so she rolled over to face the person disturbing her rest, but kept her breathing even so they would think she was still asleep. Looking through her lashes, she noticed it was Mike.

She had a good idea of what he would try if she were awake, so she laid still, hoping he would leave.

He walked across the room and pulled a chair up to the side of Megan's bed. Once he was seated, he rested his elbows on his knees and tapped his fingers in front of his scruffy chin, seeming to wonder where to begin the conversation.

Talking to her in a soft, yet admonishing voice, he said, "How could you do this to me? What were you thinking? I know you were hurt, and I'm sorry for that." He took in her bruised body and the bandages on her head.

"If you'd just woke me up, then none of this would have happened. How could you turn me into the police? Men I work with handcuffed me and put me in a cell." He shook his head in quiet disbelief.

"This is wrong, Megan. I'll have to discipline you better in the future. Sally needs a mother who knows how to obey instructions and not piss off the man of the house. I've trained you for the last ten years, and this is the way you repay me? Oh, Megan, I had such high hopes for you." Mike's voice grew louder with hate and venom. His true feelings were overshadowing any concern he might have voiced.

Listening in growing horror, Megan recoiled from his words. *What did he mean, I need to obey him? I'm not his slave. I didn't ask to be beaten. It's not my fault he fell asleep in the truck.*

On the other hand, he had spent a lot of time and effort in training me to be the wife and mother he wanted. I should have been watching for him to come home. I should have known he would be mad when I fell asleep.

Pressing the call button, Megan alerted the nurse, feeling safe in the knowledge they were just down the hall.

"Mike, I'm so sorry about this. I didn't mean for it to go this far. Can you ever forgive me?" She opened her eyes so she could see his response, hoping a nurse would arrive while she calmed him down.

Megan was convinced Mike hadn't really meant to hurt her. She needed his forgiveness because she had let him down and caused his outburst.

Mike jumped when Megan started speaking and came to stand by the bed.

"Megan, I can't forgive you until you've taken back what you've told them. Everything you tell others about me will only make matters worse for you. We can tell them you were just confused, and it was someone else who came into our house." Starting to pace beside the bed, Mike worked out a solution.

"All those lies that woman, *Allie*, has been filling your head with are just not true. You can come home and my fellow officers will help me locate this scum that did this to my wife. No one should be allowed to punish you, except for me."

Mike suddenly grabbed her wrist and held it up, seeing the call button clutched in her hand.

"What have you done, Megan?" He squeezed until the remote fell from her hand and to the floor, out of reach.

Megan began to worry as his rage built. She realized no matter what she said or did, he would never accept her back without seriously making her pay the price for coming to the hospital in the first place. The nurses might not be able to save her in time.

Mike moved his hand from her wrist to her throat as he smiled gloatingly.

"I knew this apology was too good to be true, coming from such a lying witch like you. But I took care of that before you woke up." Enjoying the terror that flooded her eyes, Mike squeezed a little more.

"There won't be anyone coming to rescue you. They're all in the break room, enjoying a short nap. I delivered some free pizzas with a little extra spice, just enough to make them sleep. I waited till they were asleep, to give us some time to have a real heart to heart talk." Mike smiled as the color faded from her face.

"I knew you were up to no good. Did you know they put me in a cell with other criminals? Guys I arrested and put in there in the past few weeks?" Shaking his head as he continued, he added, "My dear Megan, did you really think you would be safe from me after all this?"

Loosening the grip he had on her neck, it allowed her to take a deep breath so that she could answer. When she didn't, he squeezed harder, putting both hands around her neck, completely encompassing her throat. He continued squeezing until the sounds in the hall signaled an end to the sleeping nurses.

Mike hid in the bathroom as several people rushed past to check on Megan. He left the room while they were focused on her and snuck out the front door. He didn't try to hide from the cameras because if anyone asked him, he had simply gone to visit his wife.

~~~

There were only a few people housed in this hallway, and Megan was the only person who had a serious diagnosis. So the discovery of Mike's handiwork might have gone unnoticed all night if one of the nurses from the other section had not called down to ask a question.

When she didn't receive a response, she went to see what was going on and found the nurses on duty passed out in the breakroom. Pushing the emergency button to alert security and call the police, she hurried to make sure the nurses were still alive.

When the nurses from the other section were able to check on Megan, since her button had been pushed, they found her breathing hard from lack of oxygen. Even though Mike had released her before it was too late, it took a few minutes for her to breathe properly.

She had no way to gain the attention of the nursing staff when Mike slipped out the door. The staff was frantically trying to revive the passed out nurses and make sense of the chaos, so no one noticed a man leaving the building.

Megan could only whimper, but was relieved she could still breathe.

The ER doctor went straight to Megan's room. She was the only person in their small hospital that could have brought this kind of problem to their doors.

While all the others were busy trying to revive the nurses, he was the first person to see the damage Mike caused during his short visit.

The nurses from the other hall began to check on the other patients, while others ran to Megan's room once they noticed the ER doctor was heading straight for her room.

"Look at what he did to her." The ER doctor motioned a nurse closer to look at the handprint on Megan's throat. "At least he left her breathing, but just barely."

Checking her pulse and brain function for possible damage, he was amazed to see she was resting, and not unconscious.

Opening her eyes at his touch, Megan tried to speak, but only a small whimper came out. "Mike." Pointing to her ring finger, and then to her neck, she hoped the doctor would know who she was trying to say did this to her.

The police officers and sheriff's deputies arrived, adding to the confusion. Conflicting details were being given by everyone, but the main detail everyone was certain of was that Mike Butts had managed to drug the nursing staff, then attempted to kill his wife. Shaking their heads in disbelief, they finished taking statements from those who were able to give their accounts.

The charge nurse started calling in extra staff to take the place of those who were starting to regain consciousness.

For the first time ever in the small hospital's history, they instituted a security lockdown. They locked all the doors in and out of the building so only the keypads could be used. The emergency room had a lounge the injured could come in and out of, but the triage room was locked as well. There were more people in the building in the aftermath then there had been during the daylight hours with all the office staff on the premises.

Security checked the whole building to make sure Mike wasn't hiding in any of the closets or offices. Finding nothing, security considered it safe to resume operations. Each nurse that had been drugged was moved to a bed, and their recoveries were closely monitored.

Officer Grayson was called in as Megan's personal security for the rest of the night. No one would be allowed in or out of Megan's room unless Grayson gave the okay.

The crime tech people were called in to process and take pictures, while the city police officers took the nurse's statements.

The police called the pizza company to have the delivery guy return so the officers could ask him questions.

"Did you see the guy you delivered the pizza to?" Officer Stone, the backup they had called in, asked him kindly.

"Not really, dude. He came up just as I was walking in and asked, "Hey, are those the pizzas we ordered for nurses? I'll deliver them for you." When I said they were, he reached out for them and took them from me. They were paid for, dude, so I didn't worry about it." He shrugged his shoulders. "Hey, I'm just a high school student trying to earn a little extra money."

"Did you notice what he was wearing?" The officer tried to be patient, but the kid was annoying.

"Nah. Just the normal EMS uniform." The delivery guy shifted nervously between both feet.

"You said it was paid for. How did they pay for it?"

"It was a credit card. Let me call my boss and see whose name it was for ya." Pulling his phone out of his pocket, he called his boss.

"Yeah, they need the name on that delivery I did, the one for the hospital. He paused. "Okay, got it. Thanks." He then informed the officer, "It's a prepaid visa card. He has the info if you wanna trace the number." Excitement grew as the delivery guy realized there might be a way to catch the guy.

When an EMS guy had shown up at about ten with free pizza, the nurses didn't question who had sent them.

Officer Long decided to see what Officer Stone's take on the situation was from all the statements they had gathered.

"I think there's a definite problem with Mike's frame of mind, but at least he didn't kill anyone. He planned this, and now anyone who was thinking Megan was falsely accusing him of abuse will believe her. There's no way she could put those kinds of bruises on her own throat." Officer Stone was hoping they caught Mike before he could hurt anyone else.

The doctors were going back and forth between rooms, making sure all their patients were taken care of when the officers made their way to Megan's room.

"I know talking must hurt, dear, so we got you a marker board so you can answer questions for us." The doctor placed the marker in Megan's hand. As she moaned in pain, the doctor realized her left wrist, the one in the sling, was broken.

"Get me an X-ray machine in here so we can look at her hand."

Everyone left the room as the doctor looked her over. After looking at the X-ray, the doctor told Megan, "The bone in your wrist is snapped, but it won't require surgery. I believe your throat is only bruised, and will be sore for a few days. He didn't crush your windpipe, thank God. It could've been so much worse."

After setting her arm in a cast, Megan picked up the marker to try and write on the board with her good hand.

"Mike wanted 2 punish me, wanted 2 kill me. It's all my fault." Megan couldn't set aside her feelings of guilt, yet she still didn't blame Mike for his actions. After all, she had antagonized him.

The police chief and sheriff sent someone to stay in the parking lot of Allie's house so Mike couldn't do anything to harm them either. Everyone had assumed Mike wouldn't want to hurt Sally, but after his attack on Megan, they weren't taking any chances.

Having an officer at Allie's might not stop him from trying to take Sally to his hideout, but at least he would think twice before trying to abduct his daughter.

Officer Grayson took the chair Mike sat in and pulled it around the hospital bed to face the door, allowing her to see anyone that walked into the room.

~~~

When Allie got to the hospital after dropping Sally off at school, she had to show her ID to actually get into the building. Feeling anxious, she raced straight to Megan's room.

"Oh no, Megan. What happened?" Allie took one look at the bruises on her throat and knew exactly where Mike had gone when he left her house the night before. Seeing Officer Grayson sitting in the chair next to Megan's bed, she moved closer to hear the story of what had taken place the night before.

"Mike paid us a little visit, but Megan's okay. The hospital is going to start taking their security and protocols more seriously in the future." Officer Grayson grinned at the thought of pizza deliveries being scanned for any unwanted substances.

"Is anyone watching Sally while she's at school?" Allie suddenly realized if he could reach Megan in the hospital, there was nothing to stop him from kidnapping Sally from school.

"We've alerted the school officials, and they've instituted a school lockdown so we don't have an incident. When my relief gets here, I'm heading over there to work out an action plan for Sally and the other students' safety." Officer Grayson knew Mike had moved up a notch on the police watch lists from an angered husband to a violent and potentially dangerous threat to not only to his family, but anyone who got in his way.

"We're going to spend a lot of time with each other, so why don't you ladies call me Julie from now on?" Glancing at both women, Megan gave a thumbs up sign, and Allie smiled in agreement.

"Our town hasn't really had to worry about lockdown procedures before, because everyone knows everything about everyone. We always assumed it could never happen to us. So even if it's unnecessary, we get to practice how it should be done.

"We have the state troopers giving us a hand as we put out an APB to apprehend Mike. If he isn't found easily, it'll become an all-out manhunt to find him. We don't plan to give him any wiggle room to escape." Julie looked up as another officer walked into the room, tired, but alert from having been on watch all night.

"Ladies, this is Officer Clay Stone. He's staying with you until this evening, then another officer will take over. Stone, this is Megan Butts and Allie Foster. Allie's the one who's taking care of Sally while Megan recovers."

"Hello, ladies, and yes, I know my name is Clay Stone, and I've heard all of the jokes. But you're welcome to try and find one I haven't heard before." He pats Grayson on the back. "Go make sure that little girl is safe at school, all right?"

"Yes, sir." Officer Grayson lifted her hand in a teasing salute and left.

Allie hurried after her to get more details about the plan to keep Sally safe.

"Hey, Officer—I mean, Julie!" Allie called out, trying to catch up.

"Mike was outside my apartment last night. I think he was snooping around for a while, and later, he was wiggling my door knob. I had the house locked up because I had a weird feeling when I got home. Anyway, I watched all this from the peephole when he was at the door, but he soon left. I watched him walk through the parking lot and get into a car and leave. Does this mean he'll try to get Sally from my house?" Allie was scared she wouldn't be able to keep Sally safe.

"It's not very surprising since it looks like he planned this out pretty thoroughly after he got out of jail. We're assuming he has someone helping him, which at this point could be anyone here in town. He's well-known as a deputy, so he'll be able to tell people he didn't try to kill his wife in order to recruit someone to help him." Julie sighed. "Right now, we're not going to put anything on the news stations in order to prevent panic, but he knows how we operate, and with his knowledge and skill, it puts us at a distinct disadvantage."

Julie turned to face Allie fully. "I would advise you to go home and pack a few bags for you and Sally. It's probably best you stay in a hotel for the next few nights so we can protect you better. We don't want to give him an opportunity to get close to Sally.

"I have deliveries to make this afternoon and I'm finished for the week. Do you think it's safe to go back to my apartment?" Worried, Allie knew it wasn't likely for him to try anything with lots of people around.

"Honestly, I would walk in and check your apartment to make sure everything looks normal so that you feel safer. I really don't see him surfacing today. He knows we're on high alert right now. Do you have anyone you could call to drive around with you for the day?"

Allie was about to answer no, when it dawned on her that her witness protection supervisor needed to be informed of the dangerous situation she found herself in.

Sensing her hesitation, Julie felt it was important for Allie to understand how dangerous it was for her.

"Allie, Mike's going to blame you because you're helping Megan, and keeping Sally away from him."

"Is Sally safe with me?"

"Neither one of you are safe, but it's better for her to stay with someone she knows since you're now her temporary guardian. We can provide better security for both of you, rather than splitting the few officers we have in two places."

"All right. I understand, and I do have someone I can call to check the house out and make sure it's all clear. Thanks for keeping us safe."

Waving goodbye, Allie continued to her car and checked the back seat to make sure no one was hiding there. She had picked up a few tips while hanging out with the federal marshals when they handled her transfer.

Calling her contact, she explained the situation and he promised to meet her at the apartment.

Chapter 7

Allie's marshal, Keith, was waiting on the doorstep to her apartment when she arrived. In Allie's book, Keith was really good looking, but he was married. For her, that meant he was off-limits.

Keith did a walk-through while Allie hovered in the doorway.

"It's empty. Are you certain he was outside watching you last night?" Keith walked over to check out the window locks.

"Yes. I saw someone through the blinds. Then, about an hour later, the door knob rattled. He was standing there when I looked through the peephole, then took off soon after." Allie paced nervously.

"I'm going to have a tech guy come out and install some motion sensors and a camera facing both your front and back doors. Make sure you do all your changing in your bathroom for the next few days."

Allie smiled. "Shouldn't be a problem; I'm not an exhibitionist. But, I'll probably be staying wherever they decide is safe to keep Sally for the next several days. So unless I call you, there shouldn't be anyone in my apartment. I'm going to go ahead and get my bag packed up. Thanks so much for taking care of this for me."

"If you see anything, you call someone immediately. Even if it's us and it turns out to be nothing. It's better to be safe than sorry at this point," he cautioned. "I'll be back later with the tech guy. Be careful, Allie."

Taking the advice he had given her, Allie packed her bag and Sally's stuff, then deposited them into the trunk.

She needed to get the last of her orders delivered, because her customers were expecting their products. Yet today, her heart just wasn't in it.

There were days when everything was going wrong, and it could change in the blink of an eye when something good happened to balance out the bad. Today wasn't one of those days.

Answering her ringing phone, Allie didn't recognize the number. "Hello? May I help you?"

"Yes, are you the Nova Lady?"

"I am." She relaxed when she realized it was a customer.

"Well, I work up here at the funeral home, and I need to order some nail polish and lipstick." The lady spoke with precision.

Switching into her helpful mode, Allie offered her the special. "The quick dry nail polishes are on sale, two for the price of one. Did you want to try one of those?"

"It doesn't really matter if it dries fast, honey. They're not in any hurry."

As the words hit Allie's consciousness, she tried not to laugh. These polishes and lipsticks were for the dead people for their viewings.

"Oh my goodness! I guess it really doesn't matter how quickly the polish dries, then." Allie tried to contain her laughter. This unusual request was so out of the ordinary, it helped brighten her day.

This could be a great new customer for my business, Allie thought to herself.

When she'd finished collecting her order, Allie ended the call in a much better mood. "Goodbye, and I'll have everything for you next week."

This moment lifted her spirits so much, she was able to smile and enjoy taking care of her customers. While Allie didn't have a stellar selling day, at least her customers didn't have to put up with a grumpy Nova Lady.

Depositing the money from the day, before Allie headed up to the school to pick up Sally, she made a call to her boss at the Texas Teas Bar to let him know to find a replacement for the weekend. As she drove, she contemplated a diversion so that Sally didn't find out about what happened to her mother.

Arriving in the carpool lane, Allie waited until she reached the front. Sally hopped into the car as if this was their daily routine.

"Hey, kiddo. What do you say we go see a movie before we go to the hospital today?" She looked into the rearview mirror to see what Sally's reaction was.

"Sure. We never get to go to the movie theater."

"Well, today you do, kiddo." Allie was certain there would be a kid's movie playing, and probably something with a princess to boot.

~~~

The movie was okay, and Sally sang along to all the songs because it was the anniversary edition.

When it was over, they went to grab a quick bite to eat so they could make it to the hospital before visiting hours were over. Allie didn't plan to stay very long, and she wanted to protect Sally from finding out about her mom's recent injuries and how she got them.

Allie tried to prepare Sally for what she would see. "Something happened to your mommy's voice last night, and she's been hurting today. She won't sound very good, but she has a board to write on. We won't stay long once we tell her good night. Then we're going to a special place to sleep tonight. How does that sound, munchkin?"

"My daddy tried to make her go away again, didn't he? I heard the ladies at school talking about why I had to stay inside today. I thought my daddy loved us, but he needs to stop hurting my mommy. I just hate him."

Allie pulled Sally aside, into the family waiting room. Getting down to her eye level, she said, "Sally, your daddy did hurt your mommy again. He hasn't been treating her very well, but this doesn't mean he doesn't love you. I'm sure he's very upset right now, which isn't a good excuse, but we don't want to hate him, okay? He's very confused right now, and we want to find him so he can get some help and get better. We don't have to like him, but let's not hate him, all right?"

Sally burst into tears. "I'm sorry I was so bad. I'm sorry Mommy was bad. We didn't mean to be. We'll try to do better so Daddy can come back."

"Oh, sweetie." Allie could do nothing but hold her while she cried. "It wasn't your fault. It wasn't your fault, sweetheart." She kept repeating it over and over, until Sally quit crying with a hiccup.

"You and your mommy are perfect angels. Something happened to your daddy to make him do the things he's done. There's nothing wrong with you or your mommy, and I don't want you to think that way again." Allie just hoped with some time, Sally would be able to move past the feelings of guilt.

"All better?" Allie asked, leaning back to look at Sally.

"Yes," Sally answered quietly. "Can we go see my mommy now?"

"Sure thing, sweetie. I know she's waiting to see you." Holding out her hand to Sally, they made their way to Megan's room.

~~~

Megan was awake and propped up in bed. Motioning Sally over to her, they were both surprised when Sally hung back, not wanting to get close to her.

Allie walked over and lowered the side rail to give Megan a hug. When Sally witnessed that Allie didn't hurt her, she crept closer as Allie filled Megan in on all the happenings for the day. By the time Allie finished, Sally had climbed up on the bed and was studying Megan, trying to figure out if she would break.

Megan listened to Allie without trying to speak since movement still hurt, yet she wanted to assure Sally she would be all right.

"Sally, I love you. I hope you're having fun with Ms. Allie," Megan croaked out as she used her right hand to rub Sally's back.

"How was the movie? I know you love the songs." Thankfully, that was all it took for Sally to tell her everything.

"So, Officer Stone, do you know the arrangements for how we're going to get out of here?"

He motioned Allie to the other side of the room so Sally couldn't hear the details.

"We have it all ready to go in about thirty minutes. Officer Grayson will be back here shortly to stay with Megan, but we don't think Mike will try to harm her again. We're having another officer from out of town meet you at the hotel. Mike shouldn't have surveillance setup on his fellow officers, but we just want to make certain. We feel she can make it over to where you're staying without having any problems," Officer Stone patiently explained.

A little while later, Julie arrived. "Sally, give your mom a kiss and we'll take our secret ride. It'll make us invisible to everyone," Allie teased.

"No way! Really?" Sally hopped off the bed in excitement.

Picking up her backpack and duffel bag so they could leave, Sally realized she hadn't kissed her mom goodbye.

Sally went back to give her mom a quick peck on the cheek. "Later, Mom. We got places to go." She stood by the door, tapping her foot at Allie. "Well, are we going?"

Stepping closer to Megan, Allie leaned over to whisper, "I'll take care of her the best I can, but make sure you take care of yourself as well, okay?"

Megan nodded her head toward Julie, who responded with, "I'll take good care of her. Don't worry."

They walked out of the room, but instead of going out the front door, Officer Stone led them further into the hospital. They walked through many different hallways to help confuse anyone helping Mike. They finally arrived at a door facing the inside of an ambulance.

"We have arrived, ladies. The chief is hoping this will make it more difficult to be found. What do you think, Sally?" Stone gestured toward the ambulance.

"It's okay, but how are we invisible?" Sally hopped up into the back of the ambulance and started looking around.

"There aren't any windows on the side, and you both get to wear these coats so anyone looking through these windows on the back, won't be able to see who you are," Officer Stone patiently explained.

"I guess it'll do. I was really looking for something closer to fairy dust, or invisible ink for the body," Sally bickered, shaking her head in disappointment.

Stifling their laughter, Allie and Officer Stone piled into the ambulance and started putting on the EMS jackets.

Still excited about her environment, Sally asked questions. "When do you put the sirens on? How do you keep things from falling on us? Where's the blood kept?"

Thirty long minutes later, Officer Stone and the EMS team were visibly relieved to drop Allie and Sally at their destination in the neighboring town of Turner Junction.

Officer Stone escorted them to the lobby, where Officer Karen Samuels was waiting to take over the protection duty.

Feeling a sense of déjà vu, Allie followed Karen to the room setup for their protection.

Karen worked with the state police and covered a territory over two hours away. Since they were allowed to have other off-duty security jobs, the local police department had requested a female to stay with them overnight.

Since Karen didn't work in the area, it made it easy to blend in at the hotel. Allie and Karen were posing as sisters on vacation.

"So what's the plan for while we're staying here?" Allie asked curiously.

"I thought we might tour the petting zoo, located on a private ranch, then go to the butterfly gardens. Sort of a nature day. It'll be the last place Mike would think to look for us, and we can get out of the hotel for a little while tomorrow," Karen reasoned. "Oh, and I went grocery shopping so we don't have to eat out in public as much. Thankfully, the room includes a kitchen so we can make whatever we want to eat. There will be no pizza deliveries on my watch."

"I think we're going to get along just fine, Karen. We need a good sense of humor to make it through this in one piece." Allie smiled at the thought of making a new friend while she was in hiding out.

"Hey, Allie, there are lots of goodies in the cabinets. Can I have something to eat now?" Sally looked up questioningly from her explorations of the cabinets.

"I think that can be arranged. Pick out the one thing you want to have the most, then you'll have to brush your teeth." Allie didn't like being a stickler for the rules, but someone had to be the adult.

"Sally, sweetie, when you finish your snack, would you like to go ahead and take your shower so we can setup the DVD player for you?"

She sighed. "I guess so."

"Oh, I have new pj's for you to wear. I picked up a few clothing items today so we would have plenty to work with while we're here," Karen told Sally in an attempt to lighten the mood.

Relenting, Sally looked around for any sign of clothes. "What do they look like?"

"When Officer Julie told me your age, I found some pj's with princesses on them. You probably don't want to try them out, do you?" Karen waited for Sally to make the first move.

"Yeah, I could try them on for you, if you want me to." Sally looked up to see what Karen had to say.

"Let's go get them out of my room." Walking over to the adjoining room where the suitcases were laid out on the extra bed, she handed them to Sally, who rushed straight to the bathroom to take a shower, giving Allie and Karen a chance to make sure they were secure in their safety precautions.

Before Allie could ask about her concerns of Mike finding them, Karen informed her, "We have the police department here in Turner Junction making frequent drives through to look for anything suspicious. Our boss at the trooper's office made the call, so Turner Junction's officers don't even know who we're protecting. We should be safe for the moment."

"I sure hope so." Allie went to settle Sally in with her movie, leaving the door open between the rooms.

～～～

Since it was Saturday, Allie didn't have to worry about Sally going to school, making the protection detail a little easier. There was no way Allie could handle staying cooped up in a hotel room with Sally for the weekend.

"Sally, would you like to go to the pizza place and play some games?" Allie casually asked, while glancing at Karen with a grin.

"What!" Sally shrieked. "Uh, duh. We can leave now?" Sally dropped the puzzle piece she was working on and ran to the closet to get her shoes. "Ready."

"Wow! She's amazingly fast. I think she could win a marathon, don't you?" Karen teased, joining Sally at the door.

There were no sightings of Mike while Sally had a fun day filled with lots of exercise. Allie continued to look over her shoulder, though, wondering if anyone was watching them.

It was unnerving to always be on the lookout for someone to show up and ruin the day. Unaware of the tension, Sally didn't notice the extra precautions both adults were taking to avoid anything further harming this precious family.

~~~

Monday, they travelled back to see Megan at the hospital. She was feeling slightly better, and could talk with only a slight raspy sound to her voice.

"How was your weekend, honey?"

Sally spent the next hour telling Megan all about their trip and their activities. When Sally finally ran out of steam, Allie distracted her by turning on cartoons in the empty bed space while she talked to Megan.

"So what's the plan for this week?" Allie knew she needed to make some deliveries, but had no idea if they would let her return home. "I only have my Nova job until Friday, but since I didn't work this weekend, there's no way I can leave the Texas Teas Bar without help two weekends in a row."

"Well, the doctor's going to let me out by Friday. Until then, Sally's going to do her schoolwork here at the hospital during the day so you can go and take care of your business. This way, your business won't suffer, and Sally's school won't have to worry about an incident with Mike." Megan had had plenty of time over the past few days to think through her situation.

"While I hate the fact we're making everyone change their plans, I'm afraid if we try and disappear, it would only make him more upset. He would find us when the protection detail ends." Megan was so thankful Allie was there to discuss different ideas.

"We're staying at an Extended Stay hotel, so when you get out, we can make you comfortable. It has a kitchen and everything. We can wait this out. Mike won't be able to hide for long with the entire county looking for him. I'm sure you're ready to relax with Sally," Allie said sympathetically, knowing it was hard on both of them to be separated.

"We're hoping to have this wrapped up in about two weeks, since I know patience is not his strong suit. Mike will make another move soon. Things will start escalating, and he's had time to plan something big since you weren't home all weekend, so please, be careful."

Officer Stone had remained silent, simply listening, but finally interjected his thoughts on the situation. "We can provide protection on Friday while you're at work, then have a detail follow you home. With Megan and Sally at the hotel, it'll mean we can put the other escort, Julie, with you. What do you think?"

"Sounds good to me. I love Sally, but I'm not ready to become an instant mommy. I've watched enough princess movies this week to last me an entire lifetime. I don't think there are any holes left in my princess knowledge after hanging out with her." Allie smiled at Megan. "Honestly, I would love to have five minutes of silence. I had no idea a first grader could ask so many questions." Allie looked over at Sally, who was curled up in the chair, watching cartoons.

"I got a taste of that on the drive over to the protection place. I'm so glad it was Karen instead of me on your weekend detail. Sally can definitely talk," Officer Stone chuckled.

"You get used to hearing her talk, and I like having someone to take care of." Allie looked at Megan, holding one of her hands. "I haven't had many people trust me enough to protect something as precious as Sally. You have done an amazing job teaching her what love is. When she says the words 'I love you,' it's not just words. She really means them."

As Allie spoke, Megan teared up. "Thank you, Allie. I'm glad."

"All right. I'm going to go and get things sorted out at home. I'll be back this evening. Bye, Sally. Make sure you stay here and watch out for your mom, okay?"

Hearing a grunt from Sally, Megan spoke up. "Excuse me, young lady. Is that the way you respond when someone speaks to you?"

"No, ma'am. I'm sorry, Allie. I'll watch out for Mom. I'm not sure she needs it anymore, though." Scrunching up into a pouting position, Sally ignored everyone.

"It's all good, kiddo. I'll be back later." Allie left before Sally could get into more trouble.

Passing the lawyer as she headed out, Allie wondered what else he could need that they hadn't already taken care of.

~~~

Allie's apartment was clear, and the security alarm was still set when she arrived. After locking the front door and resetting the alarm, she sat down to work on her emails, and see what her team had accomplished over the weekend.

She made a list of a few ladies she needed to call to remind to submit their orders. She made a few appointments for later in the afternoon that couldn't wait until Mike was caught. Allie felt like a new woman, just being able to work on her business.

Feeling lazy over the weekend, Allie knew that watching Sally was important, but it was so different from anything she had ever done before. Knowing her time was limited this week, she got things prepped, so as she ran back and forth from the hideout and the hospital, it would be a little easier.

Sunday nights were her time to prep for the week, so it took a little longer to get things organized and ready.

Two hours later, all the books were labeled, and orders were printed and inventoried, all ready for delivery. With a sigh of relief, Allie set out to meet her first appointment at the local McDonalds.

Janet wanted to join Nova, and was able to meet today to sign up. Allie made use of the Wi-Fi connection, allowing Janet to log in and learn to navigate the Nova Lady website.

"I have some questions about Nova?" Janet spoke tentatively before Allie got ready to sign her up.

"Sure. If I don't know the answer, I'll be able to look it up for you." Allie was still new, and there was so much to learn.

Janet hesitated before saying, "Isn't this a pyramid scheme? I heard you just spend a lot of money with very little return."

"No, ma'am. In this business, what you put into it will be what you get out of it. Nova is not a get rich overnight scheme. If you work hard and are consistent, then you'll see the rewards. We don't pressure people into signing up. In fact, if you were to move higher than I am with your hard work, there is nothing keeping you from succeeding," Allie explained confidently.

"Oh, thank goodness. I've heard lots of horror stories this week." Janet spoke with relief.

"Here are a few practical ideas for customer growth." Allie began to explain the process while Janet took notes.

"So, did I answer all your questions about becoming a Nova Lady?" Allie wanted to make sure Janet was comfortable moving forward.

"Yes. I already have several ladies who want books and can't wait until I can bring them over this afternoon." Janet's excitement began to show through.

"That's wonderful, Janet. You're already working your business! Remember, passing out books is only part of the process. You have to follow up and get their orders. Otherwise, you don't make any money." Shaking hands and giving Janet her startup package, Allie realized she hadn't thought about Mike during the whole setup.

Helping others was important to Allie; she didn't sell Nova just to benefit from the money she made. It was the sense of accomplishment she felt when other ladies started working to reach their life goals.

Some would take her up on the offer, then never do anything with it, while others, with a little encouragement, were able to accomplish more than they had ever thought possible.

It was like wearing two different hats all the time—boss and mentor. The ability to show other ladies how to make their business work while allowing them to support their families was something Allie really enjoyed.

Allie loved meeting new people, just like with Megan. Someone could change your life by a chance encounter.

She had two more appointments scheduled, so after Janet left, she refilled her cup of soda and got the next startup kit ready. When an hour passed and no one showed up, she texted the new girl, Beth.

Allie: It's the Nova Lady. Are you still meeting me today?

Beth: Sorry, forgot. Next time?

Allie: Let's try for Wednesday. Same time, okay?

Beth: No, I don't think I want to do it after all.

Allie: Let me know if you change your mind. Thanks.

It was always disappointing when someone stood her up, but Allie was certainly familiar with people who disappointed her in life.

Allie settled in to wait for her next appointment by working on her laptop and sending out emails. She also updated the group page so her team could stay updated on where meetings and events were taking place while she was out with Megan.

Standing up as the next appointment came in, Allie introduced herself to Betty.

"Hey, Betty. Are you ready to get started on your Nova adventure?" Allie held out her hand as Betty took the seat across from her.

"Absolutely! So how do does this work?" Betty asked excitedly.

A few questions later, Allie had determined that Betty's goal was to earn enough money to take the family on vacation.

"Betty, your goal is totally possible, and with the number of names you've been writing down, I think you'll have enough saved up for your vacation very quickly." Allie could see the potential in Betty as a motivated Nova Lady, and she wanted to keep her challenged with bigger goals.

"What would you do with twice as much money, Betty?"

"Well, we have an older car that we need to replace. It's paid for, and we don't have money for a new car note." Betty's excitement began to build.

Allie couldn't help but feel Betty's excitement as well. "If you take what you've started here and work on it, we can help you make your goal of a new car by next year."

She finished up her day by leaving books in a few new places and went home to collect the order waiting on her doorstep.

Amazed that her packages were sitting there waiting for her when she got home, Allie couldn't help but be thankful for small town honesty. Unlike living in New York, where she had four locks on the door, she didn't have to worry about her deliveries disappearing from the doorstep.

"Now to bag up the orders for tomorrow so I can get everything delivered. Ugh, I forgot we have to drive over from Turner Junction, and I have no idea how long it'll take to drive from the hotel and back up to the hospital. Well, I think I've done all I can for today. I'll just have to be flexible with things tomorrow."

Grabbing extra clothes, Allie reset the alarm and headed up to the hospital to collect Sally for their drive back to the hotel. Tonight's transportation would be in an empty coroner's vehicle, so there wasn't an established pattern Mike could follow. Allie could only imagine the questions from Sally about their ride for the night.

~~~

When Allie walked into the room, she instantly spotted Julie playing cards with Sally.

"Sally's getting her work assignments tomorrow, and will be busy working on those while you're at work. I know she's just so excited, and it'll give her something constructive to do during the next few days." Megan was glad Sally would be able to stay current with her classwork while they waited for Mike to make a move.

Megan's lawyer, Mr. Greenley, stopped by with dinner. He arrived dressed in his casual clothes, and looked like he was going to stay awhile. He didn't look terrible in his comfy clothes, either. Allie raised an eyebrow at Megan, with a, 'What's going on between you two?' look.

"Mark's keeping me company tonight since I found out he's a fan of reality shows. He thought I could use some company since I wouldn't be going anywhere for a while." Megan felt the need to explain since Allie was obviously curious.

Allie turned toward Mark. "I'm glad you're keeping her mind off everything that's going on. The worst thing someone can do is sit around and wonder about the what-ifs. Thanks for keeping her company."

She winked at Megan. "Now, you two have a good evening, and I'll see you tomorrow morning. Don't stay up too late." Allie walked over to the door as Sally gave her mom a good night kiss.

Megan had anticipated questions about Mark hanging out with her. He was just a nice guy, and she wasn't taking his interest personally, because she wasn't really all that pretty.

With all her bruises, she must have looked like something out of a horror film. She'd been lucky to find Mike in the first place. Not many men were willing to marry a homely woman to begin with. Megan knew Mark was trying to keep her mind off the possibility that Mike could sneak back into the hospital. Certain Allie would give her grief about Mark's presence the next morning, Megan was determined to enjoy the evening and put the rest out of her mind for now.

Chapter 8

The next morning, Allie was thankful for another uneventful night, and was ready to take Sally back to the hospital to spend the day. Julie volunteered to walk with Sally to see the newborn babies and give Megan some time to catch up with Allie.

"The entire police department, troopers, and deputies he worked with have been searching for almost a week and haven't found Mike yet." Megan continued keeping tabs on everything when each shift changed.

"That's what really worries me. I feel like he's planning something to get even with us for causing him all this trouble. He could be holed up anywhere. Did Mike have a best friend?"

"Not really. He hung out with the guys from work. The police are looking into identifying any of his close friends, and where his favorite camping sites are. I told them he didn't go on overnight trips very often. There were a few camping trips over the years, but not many, and he went to poker night every week." Megan shrugged, feeling defeated.

Allie hated to ask the question, but felt it was worth considering. "Did Mike have a woman he was seeing on the side? I know you don't think so, but there were times when he worked a lot of "overtime," right?" Allie said, using air quotes to convey her message.

"Yes," Megan answered very quietly. Her throat was still healing, but the damage to her vocal cords was still noticeable.

"He could have been with someone and you didn't notice because he was supposedly at work, so you wouldn't have suspected anything."

Megan grimaced. "At this point, anything is possible, but the guys he hung out with haven't come forward with any information, so there's no telling if he did or not."

Starting to mentally berate herself, she almost missed the sly smile on Allie's face when she asked, "So what's up with Mark Greenley? Is he rescuing you from your thoughts again tonight?"

"For your information, he's coming over. I really think he feels guilty he didn't keep me safe from Mike. I know there's no way it was his fault, but he feels responsible since Mike was able to get out on bail," Megan quipped.

Allie didn't want Megan to be embarrassed or defensive, so she quickly changed the subject when the door opened and Sally entered the room.

~~~

Allie went to pick up the deliveries that were ready at her apartment. It was a smaller order this week, since it was the off week for paydays for her customers.

Deciding to check in with Kevin, Allie gave him a call while she put her clothes in the apartment's small laundry room.

"Hey, Kevin. How are those cameras working out for us?"

"So far so good, Allie, and hello to you too," Kevin answered with a chuckle. "Nothing in or out, so if this continues, I don't see why you can't come home when you're ready."

"Oh, wonderful. I'm so relieved. I'm ready to return home and sleep in my own bed again. Thanks for looking out for me. Catch you later."

Allie carried her clothes out of her apartment and over to the laundry room to start a load.

Filling the washers with clothes and detergent, she placed the quarters in the slots as she mentally tried to figure out what to do next. *I think I'll go run a few deliveries over to the bank. I should be back before anyone needs to use the washers again.*

Returning an hour and a half later, Allie was relieved that no one seemed to be waiting on the washers. She began to load her clothes into the dryer when she found one load had already been moved over for her. This was a typical occurrence with apartment dwellers, since there were only a small amount of washers and dryers available.

Grimacing, she noticed there must have been something red left behind in the washer since the clothes she pulled out had a red tint to them. "Ugh!" she exclaimed.

"Now my whites are a lovely shade of red. Nothing I can do except dry them and have a new shade of towels." Placing the quarters in the slot, Allie then noticed a red liquid running out of the dryer door with the clothes she hadn't moved herself.

"What the hell is that?" She quickly called Kevin to come and investigate because it looked suspiciously like blood. As she walked over to switch out the other loads while she waited, Allie was greeted with a horrific sight.

Her other washer had parts of a dripping dead rabbit inside of it. She opened the lid of the next washer, which was full of work clothes, and found rabbit's feet. Blood was sprinkled over the clothing in both washers.

Taking out her phone, she took pictures to stay busy until Kevin got there.

Unsure if renter's insurance would cover vandalism, Allie was relieved when Kevin walked through the door.

"So I guess Mike made an appearance today." In a way, Allie was glad Mike had finally made a move.

"Well, I wouldn't be so sure. I alerted the police, but since we have no proof as to who vandalized your laundry, we can't assume anything unless there's evidence. We both know Mike is too smart to leave any behind. We'll still look." Kevin wished he could be more helpful, but sometimes the legal system was frustrating.

"I only did a few loads of mine and Sally's clothes. I think I can throw them away once the police are done. I don't want a reminder of today." Allie was thankful it was only three loads of clothes, and not all her dirty laundry.

Going back to her apartment while Kevin waited for the police, Allie packed new clothes and anything extra she thought they might need for the next few days. There was no way she wanted to spend the night by herself after what she'd seen today.

It was still early in the afternoon, and there was no reason to head to the hotel yet, so it looked like she would spend a few hours with Sally in Megan's room.

Mike's disturbing message had made it impossible to get any work done. He hadn't forgotten about his family, and was just waiting patiently until they let their guard down to make a move.

~~~

On the other side of town, on a rural dirt road, a truck was making its way to the tree line, kicking up quite a cloud of dust since there had been so little rain this spring. The man driving the truck kept on driving long after the road ended, even though there were only two ruts in the dirt to follow down the seldom used path. The truck continued another mile until it was hard to see where the path turned as the trees started to close in, obscuring anything but the forest. The path became narrower, making it almost impassable as he pulled up to a cabin. The man in the truck got out cautiously, announcing his presence as he approached.

"Mike, I'm here! Don't shoot!" He collected a few bags of groceries and a case of beer from the truck bed before starting for the porch.

In the growing dusk, a light outlined a shadow in the doorway. The cabin had no electricity, and was completely off the grid. The safest place for Mike to hide out while the entire county searched for him.

"Well, did they get my little gift?" Mike asked of the guy carrying all the groceries.

"Yeah, they did. You should've seen how scared they were. They're constantly looking over their shoulders now. I got the pictures you asked for, but I was afraid I wouldn't get to take them." He nervously ran his fingers through his hair, feeling unsure about what Mike would've done if he had failed.

"That woman left the hospital this morning and started moving around, so it was easy to follow her. I took a few pictures when she went to take her clothes out of the washers. She found the rabbit, but she didn't call out or anything. She called some guy, and they called the police together."

"Did they wonder how I got in to put the dead rabbits in the washer and dryer?" Mike grabbed the beer from him and started putting the groceries in an old ice box. Opening a beer for himself, he headed toward the porch, leaving his errand boy to follow.

"Well, they have everything staked out, so it would be hard for you to have done it, but I put the tracker on her car so I would know where she was while I was fixing her clothes. Evidently, she just planned to run errands, so it left plenty of time for me to sabotage her laundry and get back on watch."

He watched Mike, looking for a sign of approval for the methods he was using.

"Were you able to see Sally? Was she with that woman?" Mike asked gruffly.

His friend fidgeted while he tried to explain. "No, Mike. Man, I'm sorry, but when she left the hospital, there was no sign of Sally. I listened at the briefing this morning, and the only information mentioned was that Sally wouldn't be returning to school until this was resolved. They're really scared of what you'll do next. I don't know what they think you'll do to your own daughter. I mean, really, if Megan hadn't tried to escape what she had coming to her, then you wouldn't be in this mess."

Listening to him ramble on, Mike realized this was the very reason the local and state police hadn't caught him yet. They were just too incompetent to deal with someone who had real police training. He knew since his little visit to Megan's hospital room, they'd been chasing their tails, trying to find out where he was hiding.

"Do you have anything else you want me to do tomorrow, Mike? I could plant a bomb in the woman's car so it takes her out for being so meddlesome."

"Not yet, dude. You've done such a great job, and I don't want you to get caught, or you might have to come hide out here with me." Mike threw him a bone of appreciation. "You know, if we do too much too soon, the police will figure out what we're up to. I don't want to cause any trouble for you, friend. Let's see what they do tomorrow. I would love to see those pictures, though. Put a new SD card in the camera and I'll check them out later."

Mike wanted to keep his friend happy, but not give him more information than he really needed. He got up and began walking toward the truck, and his obedient man-puppy followed.

"You head on home. Otherwise, your wife will be wondering where you are. I know you're getting lots of overtime, but we don't want to give her any reason to check up on you, right?"

Mumbling, he climbed into the truck and promised to text Mike if anything new developed.

Mike felt relief when his bumbling helper left. He knew the odds were almost nil that he would be able to get his family back.

He planned to punish Megan by making her paranoid. Throwing his half-drunk beer against the cabin wall in anger, Mike started to pace anxiously, and began to rant.

"If Megan won't come back home, then my only choice is to take Sally from her. Not that I really want to take care of a kid for the rest of my life, but the devastation it would cause

Megan would be worth it. I can always leave Sally somewhere later on if she gets to be too much trouble. There are always places for a man with my kind of connections to go off the grid."

"I don't want that horrible woman to have my daughter any longer than necessary. As for that bitch who's helping my wife, I have special plans for her, but it'll take some planning to get her away from all the police protection surrounding her at the moment."

Mike methodically went through his plan to scare Megan and her bitch friend.

"I'll stalk and terrorize them. It'll keep Megan and the cops chasing their tails, looking for me on cameras. The laugh is on all of you, because I've been less than ten miles away from that woman all day."

Mike sat back on the porch and grabbed another beer to help clear his head and come up with a better plan to get back what was rightfully his.

~~~

The doctor came in to check on Megan's progress.

"Well, it looks like we have a crowd today. Let's see how you're doing. Talk to me so I can hear your vocal cords."

"I'm feeling better, and the nurses helped me take a shower this morning, so I feel clean as well." Megan was starting to get antsy the longer she had to stay in the hospital bed.

"Perfect. Your voice is sounding better, and the bruises are starting to fade from your throat. I think we can send you to the hotel later this afternoon. You'll have to take it easy and come in on Monday for a checkup, unless something happens. I think you'll recover better when you're staying with Sally. What do you think, young lady?" The doctor turned so he could see Sally's expression.

"My mommy can come and live with me again? Oh, goodie." Sally ran across the room and gave the doctor a fierce hug.

"I think this means we should go back to Karen and get some shopping done so that we can relax when your mom gets to the hotel. Want to help me buy some clothes for your mom to wear?"

"Yeah, shopping. Can we shop till we drop? I've been dying to do that my whole life. Please?" Sally bounced up and down in front of Allie.

"We'll see, but we have to get a move on." Herding Sally out, Allie waved goodbye to Megan as they found a covert way out of the hospital. "See you in a little while."

~~~

At the store, Sally helped pick out the pj's for Megan.

"Let's get Mommy these." Sally held up a Minnie Mouse set and a Tinkerbell set. "She'll love them, I just know it."

Allie and Karen exchanged an amused look. "How about some soft T-shirts and shorts?" Karen walked over to the ladies' section.

"Oh, okay, but can I please get one set?" Sally pleaded.

"Yeah, but you'll have to choose which ones you think she'll like the best." Allie wondered if patience was something one could only acquire with a mommy card.

111

"I think we have enough stuff for now, but we need to go back to the room and clean up so your mom will be able to rest." Karen was happy to see Sally so excited.

"Have you missed having your mom to hang out with?" Sally nodded in reply.

As they cleaned up the hotel room, Karen and Allie discussed what other preparations they needed to make.

"We should put Megan in here on one bed and let Sally sleep in the other bed. We can both sleep in the other room, and that'll help both of them adjust to each other better." Karen was trying to keep everything secure and comfortable at the same time.

"I agree. We can hear everything and block off the hotel door in their room so if someone wants to come through it, we'll hear what's going on from our room. I'm looking forward to the slumber party with the both of you." Allie was glad Karen had become another friend in the process of looking out for Megan and Sally.

Restocking the cabinets, Karen explained what they were going to do as they searched for Mike. "Both departments are going to continue to search for Mike. They're going to keep the hospital on security lockdown so Mike won't find out that Megan was discharged. It should give you a little bit of extra protection."

"Most of these precautions seem a little excessive, don't you think?" Allie wasn't in law enforcement, but it seemed that Mike still had the upper hand.

"Considering Mike is smart and knows all our procedures, they're trying to keep him off guard, hoping he'll mess up so we can catch him."

"I just hope no one else gets hurt because he can't find Megan," Allie whispered so that Sally wouldn't hear."

"Maybe we can wrap this up soon for everyone's sake, and without any more injuries." Karen went into the other room to finish preparing for Megan's arrival.

~~~

It was late on Wednesday when the car driving Megan arrived at the hotel. Officer Karen went down to help her from the car, through the lobby, and up to their rooms.

Megan looked exhausted from the trip, so they helped her straight into the bed. The hospital had given her scrubs to wear, since her original clothing had been covered in blood, making it necessary to cut them off her when she arrived.

Having been in bed for almost a week, Megan was feeling better, but needed more recovery time before she was out of bed for more than a bathroom trip.

"Do you need some water, Mom? More pillows? We have all kinds of things to eat, and the DVD player is ready when you want to watch a movie." Sally couldn't contain her enthusiasm about her mother's arrival.

Sitting on the edge of the bed, Megan tried to regain her breath from the walk to their room. "Sally, darling, I could use a couple pillows to prop me up."

Racing to the other room, Sally returned with as many pillows as she could hold and placed them behind her mother.

"Here, I'll pull your shoes off so you can lean back on the pillows." Sally jerked Megan's shoes off, proud of her accomplishment.

"Thank you, darling. Now, I need a gentle hug before I lay down." Sally stood to the side and gave her a quick squeeze. "I love you, munchkin. We can have some fun once I've rested up, okay?"

"Okay, Mom. I'm going to go watch cartoons in Karen's room. You get some sleep." Hopping out of the room, Sally disappeared.

Visibly wilting, Megan groaned as she pulled her legs up on the bed and leaned back. With a smile, Megan was asleep moments later, as a slight snore filled the room.

~~~

When Megan woke, it was dark in her room, but she could hear the sounds of a gameshow playing in the other bedroom where the girls were loudly calling out the answers.

Before Megan could get up to join them, the sound of a phone ringing brought everyone into Megan's room.

Seeing all their confused faces at the sound, Megan pointed to the pile of things she had brought in with her.

"Uh, I think it's in my bag over there." She tried to act nonchalant about a phone call.

Julie, who had replaced Karen on duty, was posing as another sister who had joined them on vacation. People didn't ask questions or pay much attention to a group of women hanging out. Julie walked over and picked up the bag and handed it to Megan.

Fishing the phone out as it continued to ring, Megan answered. "Hello? Sorry it took so long to answer, I was asleep. Hold on just a sec." She motioned to her audience. "It's

Mark. I promised to call, I just didn't think I would sleep so long."

Herding Julie and Sally back into the other room, Allie challenged her. "You haven't heard the last of this, missy." Grinning, Allie pulled the door shut to give Megan some privacy.

Still too tired get up and go into the other room after her call ended, Megan called out. "I'm off the phone." She knew the ladies in the next room were close to the door, trying to listen in on the conversation.

Curiosity pulled the ladies back to see why Megan had a new phone.

"So, just calling to check on you, huh?" Allie started the discussion by probing for information as she entered the room."

"Well, Mark thought I should have a prepaid phone in case we needed to call him or the police. It won't be as easy to trace as hotel numbers would be."

"Oh, I think someone is being very helpful, don't you?" Allie grinned at Julie as she crossed over to the small kitchen.

With a slight blush on her cheeks, Megan defended Mark. "He was just checking to make sure we were all settled in, and there hadn't been any problems. I assured him we were fine, just tired."

Sally came back in the room, distracting Megan from their conversation by climbing into the bed with her.

Allie motioned Julie into the small kitchenette so they could speak without Sally or Megan overhearing.

"I think we need to find out what Mark is up to with our Megan. I think he's smitten with her. What do you think?" Allie whispered.

"He was there most of the time, just making sure she had company. Not that I wasn't right there if she needed me. I mean, you would think she'd be skittish around another guy, but who am I to assume?" Julie agreed.

"Do you really think he's a good guy? I mean, I would hate for her to get taken advantage of in a new situation before she can recover emotionally from the old one."

"He's from a really great family. They're well-known in the community for helping others, and are dedicated Church goers." Leaning on the kitchen bar, Julie continued to whisper. "If he can give her enough space to work through the emotions and recovery, then I think it might be okay. She has a long road ahead of her and is still in shock from everything that's happened to her."

Julie looked to see if Megan could hear them before continuing in a hushed tone. "I don't think Mike's done yet. The stalking and threats could get worse. He's overconfident and self-righteous, which is why he was never promoted, even though he had all the right credentials."

"Mark will have to be very patient and let her grow her own wings before she'll be able to accept any type of relationship. They may stay friends for a long time."

Allie was thankful she had help to keep an eye on the developing relationship.

"I think Megan is still so naïve. She won't see what he's offering, then she'll be embarrassed that she didn't see it coming. It should be fun to watch and see how this progresses." Allie snickered at the thought of Megan's face when she realized that Mark was interested in more than just a friendship.

"Well, he seems okay so far, but I'm not a very good judge of men either." Allie had only been on a few dates since moving to Texas. She didn't feel any sparks with any of the guys she had gone out with.

"Maybe we don't need to dream about finding the fairytale. I'm not sure those guys really exist. I've dated a few nice guys, but who knows what they're really like when you get them home, right?" Julie wasn't ready to give up hope, but she did have a cynical view of reality.

"This whole situation is one reason I haven't tried to look very hard. I've never really had a good role model. My foster families weren't horrible, but they didn't win the foster family of the year either. I just learned to stay out of the way so I wasn't sent to a new home, you know?" Allie hadn't told anyone about her past, and if she was going to make friends, she had to let some walls down.

"Well, I hope this guy doesn't hurt her, but how anyone could hurt her worse than Mike has is hard to imagine. Anything would have to be better than him, right?"

Allie shrugged in response to Julie's question, as Sally ran over to see what they could eat.

"Mommy's ready to eat, and I told her I would make her a peanut butter and jelly sandwich. She loves it when I make them for her." Sally started getting out the ingredients they would need.

Seeing Megan cringe at Sally's statement, Julie helped with the preparations.

"Why don't I make us grilled cheese instead so that we have a hot meal to eat, and we can do those later if we get snacky, okay?" Julie crossed her fingers, hoping Sally would go for it.

Pausing in her efforts to gather the supplies, Sally tilted her head while making her decision. "I guess we could do that for tonight." Sally agreed. "I do love grilled cheese."

"Sally, why don't we work on getting the movie ready and push the two beds next to each other for a big couch for all of us to sit on?" Allie tried to distract Sally from the kitchen activates so Julie could work in peace.

The consensus was to watch an old movie while they ate dinner. They chose *You've Got Mail* since it was more age appropriate for Sally as well.

By the time it was over, both Sally and Megan were asleep. Allie tucked them in, while Julie did a check to make sure everything was still secure.

"Hey, Julie. Since it's quiet, I think I'm going to take a bath and soak for a while."

Laughing, Julie agreed. "Hey, it's hard to have any quiet time with that small one around. Go ahead. I'm going to change and watch the news for a while."

Escaping to the bathroom, Allie hoped the warm water would help soak out all her stress. Her thoughts reflected her adventures so far.

"I hope they let me work Friday night, because I'm going to go crazy cooped up with three other women, even if one is only half-sized." She smiled to herself. *"Sally's size doesn't stop her from having full-sized emotions. House arrest sounds*

lovely if it means I can have a day all to myself again. I hadn't realized I excluded the people around me, and kept the ones who could be friends at arm's length."

Allie interacted well with people, but when she was at home for the night, it was lonely for a person without family connections.

"Geeze, lighten up, Foster. It's not like I have a cat, or that I've started a collection of cats to fit in with my old lady lifestyle. I do need to change some of my habits to include more friends and the time to spend with them."

Julie knocked, interrupting Allie's pity party. "Allie? Were you planning to stay in there all night? I was hoping you could stay out here while I showered. It's almost midnight."

"Sure, I'll be right out." She jumped up, pulling the plug as she got out. She dried off quickly and threw on her jammies.

She opened the door as she finished toweling her hair dry. "I'm sorry. It was so peaceful, I got carried away by Calgon." Allie tried to say it with a straight face, but didn't succeed.

Julie burst out laughing, but quickly covered her mouth when she remembered the sleepers in the next room.

"I remember those old commercials, 'Calgon, take me away,' and then the lady would put her hand on her head and sigh. Oh, thanks, girl. That takes me back."

Allie realized this time would always be remembered as the time when she made some real friends. It might not be a fun time, but these roots would last beyond the crisis they were going through.

Allie checked on the other room while Julie was in the shower and got into bed. She was sound asleep when Julie got out of the shower and didn't hear anything until Sally jumped on her bed the next morning.

Chapter 9

Trying to be considerate of Megan, Allie and Julie let Sally stay in their room for most of the morning.

Since Sally had the undivided attention of the two ladies, her homework was quickly finished, and Allie started her on a puzzle, but the distraction didn't last very long with the three of them working on it.

Sally couldn't wait any longer and snuck into Megan's bed, showering her with wake up kisses.

After stretching and sitting up, Megan was ready to try the shower. Allie helped her, while Julie and Sally got lunch ready. The four girls spent the day watching movies and painting nails, just having a regular girls day in.

Other than a few calls to make sure they were okay, nothing eventful happened.

By Friday, they were sick of each other, and were glad when Officer Karen showed up to switch out with Julie.

Allie had already gathered her things so she could head back with Julie and catch up on her Nova work before heading to the bar later that evening.

Hugging Megan, Allie admonished Sally. "Take care of your mom, and don't let her get too tired. Bye, kiddo." Kissing Sally on the head, they left them in Karen's capable hands

When Karen opened the hotel room door, she was attacked with hugs from Allie and Julie as they quickly left the room.

"Glad to see you too," Karen called out as the door shut on their fleeing backs.

The car ride over to the hospital was comfortable, with Allie and Julie discussing the details needed for their adventure with work that evening.

"Do you think Mike will follow me from my apartment?" Allie felt a little apprehensive since the incident with the washer and dryer.

"The police chief and sheriff are hoping that if you follow your regular schedule, it'll lead him out in the open so we can catch him. Since he hasn't found where Megan and Sally are staying, there's a good chance he'll try to follow you. That's why I'll be across the street, on duty. We want him to show up so we can finish this manhunt." Julie hoped they could wrap this up and go back to normal.

Allie felt like skipping to the car. She was so excited to head home, even if it was only for a few hours.

Julie continued to observe her surroundings before taking Allie up to the hospital to pick up her vehicle. Julie followed Allie to her house and walked through it with her to make sure it was still safe.

"I'll stay inside my apartment until you come back at five to take me to work." She crossed her heart. "Promise."

Laughing as she left, Julie waved goodbye.

Resetting the security alarm, the first thing Allie did was to spin in circles. "Wheeee!" So excited to be back in her quiet house, she took a moment to let it sink in.

Settling down to business, she started answering emails and returning the phone calls that had accumulated during her absence. Explaining the situation in an e-mail to her team, she let them know who to call in case of a lipstick emergency while she was out of pocket.

Allie made herself lunch and took a nap. Sleeping so soundly, she almost didn't hear the alarm she'd set to get ready for work at the bar.

Feeling refreshed and ready to tend bar for the night, Allie got dressed and put on her makeup while waiting for her escort to show up.

Restless, she cleaned out the fridge and collected the trash to help fill the time until Julie showed up.

Julie finally called. "Hey, I'm out here."

"All right. I'm going to carry the trash around back to the dumpster." Allie picked up her keys and backpack with her wallet and a change of clothes.

When the alarm beeped, she grabbed the trash and locked up.

Returning to the front parking lot, she checked the back seat and glanced under the car to make sure there weren't any surprises. Waving to Julie, Allie went to work, parking her car under the street lamp, making it easily visible to everyone.

Thankful to be back at work, Allie felt sorry for Julie who had to stay out in her car across the street, watching for any sign of Mike. She felt safe in her work environment. While a bar could be considered by some to be a hostile workplace, the Triple Teas Bar was more like home to those employed there. Allie hadn't grown up with that family feeling, so it was nice to be accepted by the locals who came by to hang out on the weekends.

Waving off everyone's concern over her absence, Allie was glad when the crowd grew too big for in-depth conversations. They were short staffed, so the night was more hectic, causing her to pull double duty as bartender and waitress.

Around ten o'clock, Allie noticed a group come in and take over the pool tables that had been vacated a short time earlier. Having a mix of guys and girls in the group, Allie didn't pay much attention until she turned to get the last person's order and slammed straight into his chest.

~~~

Justin was distracted by Stephanie, who was pulling him toward the pool table when he collided with Allie.

Reaching out to steady her, he apologized. "I'm so sorry, miss."

Allie jerked back as though he had shocked her. Unsure of her crazy reaction to him, Allie continued back to the bar, while glancing over her shoulder to keep an eye on him.

Justin was watching Allie as she balanced her tray, moving away from him.

As they made eye contact, Allie mouthed a belated, "Thank you."

Justin took up a stool in the corner, watching all the activity going on around him.

"Quit sitting over in the corner and come play with us, Justin." Stephanie continued to gravitate to his side, giving him all her attention.

"I'm fine here, thanks." Justin didn't move from his spot on the stool.

After her third attempt to pull him into the conversation, Justin, feeling frustrated, stood and told Stephanie, "Let's go outside for a minute."

"Sure. No problem." Giggling as she took his extended arm, Stephanie was overjoyed to have his full attention.

Justin was the perfect guy, single and handsome. A date with him was the coveted position all the ladies in town were vying for.

She almost ran into him when he stopped short just outside of the doors. Stephanie's hopes dwindled when she saw the look on his face wasn't an invitation to dinner. When he frowned down at her, she realized that he wasn't interested in her and was going to let her down easy.

Taking the offensive, Stephanie started in on Justin.

"Ugh. Don't tell me I'm not good enough for you. What do you guys really want in a lady?" Placing her hands on her hips, she shook her head in disgust. "Seriously! I work out, and there's not an ounce of fat on this body." She ran her hand in a downward motion to emphasize her words. "I do volunteer work, and even help organize church socials. What else could a guy like you want in a woman?" Nervously tapping her foot, Stephanie waited for his answer.

"Well, since you asked me…" Justin couldn't believe the anger he was getting from Stephanie. "I'm looking for someone who doesn't do good deeds just for show or social status. I want a lady I can work with, not someone to place on a pedestal to take down and dust off once a week." There was no nice way to let Stephanie down from her very high expectations, so Justin continued. "I don't have anything against you or how you look. There are lots of guys who follow every move you make. I'm just looking for someone I have a connection with, and it hasn't happened with you. I'm sorry."

Moving to leave, Justin touched her arm gently. "Stephanie, you're really nice, but I think there's some other guy out there for you. I'm not trying to pity or patronize you, but I don't think I'm what you're looking for."

Justin hated letting someone down, but there was never a good way to let a girl know she didn't fit the notion of his dream girl.

Looking at him in disbelief, Stephanie reached up and slapped him hard across the face.

"Maybe next time, you'll think before you lead a girl on like that." Turning, she raced back inside to avoid facing him again.

Not surprised she had responded that way, Justin rubbed his face. He went back inside, only instead of returning to his friends, he headed for the crowded bar.

It would be better to give Stephanie a moment to calm down before they were in the same social circle again.

A spot opened at the far end of the bar, and Justin claimed it quickly before someone else could.

Hearing a rippling laugh, Justin followed the sound and found the girl he had collided with earlier standing behind the far end of the bar.

Pete was telling her a story. Since Pete was in his seventies, it was nice to see her paying attention to an old man, even if there wasn't anything in it for her. Pete wasn't known for his large tips, so the attention Allie was paying him seemed genuine.

The evening took on a new look as Justin realized there might be a way to salvage the evening after all.

~~~

Justin spent the next two hours watching her clean up and take orders. She genuinely seemed to enjoy her job, as she flirted harmlessly with the guys and gals around her. She graciously turned down many offers to dance from the patrons on a regular basis.

Working a mixture of waitressing and bartending around the crowd, she easily changed hats, depending on what was needed. He was impressed as he watched her work the room.

He accidentally made eye contact with Stephanie from across the room. A sneer crossed her face as she realized he was checking the waitress out. Deciding it was a good time to visit the boy's room, Justin motioned he would be back to the other girl at the bar and leaned his stool against the counter.

Waiting as long as he could to return, Justin slowly made his way into the room, hoping Stephanie and his friends were gone. Sneaking around the corner, he let out a sigh of relief to find the pool table was empty.

Catching sight of his group heading out the door, he paused until they were gone before resuming his seat.

"Did you want another beer?" Hearing her voice at his elbow saved Justin from searching the room for her.

"Yeah, thanks." Justin wasn't sure how to start up a conversation with her.

"What's your name, ma'am?"

"Allie. Oh, the girl you were hanging out with said to give you a message if you ever came out from hiding in the bathroom."

Allie was well acquainted with his type—good looking and charming, until the next morning when they wanted nothing else to do with a girl.

"She said she hoped you could find the right type of girl to take care of you. God only knows you'll need someone to ride in and knock you off that black stallion you're so proud of.'" Allie started to move away when Justin spoke.

"She was mad I wouldn't take her out on a date. I wouldn't because we had nothing in common. She just wanted to be seen with me so others would like her as well."

Ugh! Way to go. Justin mentally slapped himself. *Put another girl down, and she'll totally want to date you. Smooth, man."*

"Well, don't feel too bad. She needs to take the stick out of her butt, but that's just my opinion. You can't force someone to like you. It's either there or it's not." Allie shrugged. "Here's your beer. It's on me." She pulled some money from her apron and placed it in the register, moving on to another customer.

Allie glanced at the guy again. *Obviously, the girl's perfect body wasn't this guy's dream. Although, she is gorgeous and built, but who knows why he wasn't interested. Oh well, not my problem."*

Trying not to stare at her the rest of the night was more difficult than Justin thought it would be.

The other girl replaced Justin's beer. "Last call, dude. By the way, Allie isn't really the type to pick up someone at her workplace. Better luck next time."

Beginning to feel like a stalker, Justin took the hint when Allie never made it back up to his area of the bar. Leaving a few extra dollars for a tip, he went outside and leaned against the wall to clear his head.

Trying to think of a plausible excuse to ask her out, it was hard to think when he just kept repeating his part in the horrible conversation with her.

Not realizing the parking lot was clearing out, Justin was lost in thought when the bouncer, Stan, walked Allie out to her car, making sure she was inside before turning to find Justin standing there.

"You need to go home or I'll call the cops. Which option do you want, bub?" Stan was a large man, and he blocked Justin's view of Allie when he placed his hands on his hips.

"Oh, sorry. Got lost in thought. I'll head home now. Didn't mean any harm." Justin started toward his car, but stopped when both men heard a muffled cry.

Allie's car revved up, then slammed into the dumpster.

Shocked at the scene unfolding before them, Stan screamed Allie's name as he raced toward the accident.

The car was sitting still, but Stan and Justin were startled when the back driver's side door opened and a man jumped out.

"I checked the back seat. Where did that guy come from?" Stan muttered to himself as the man took off running into the night.

A truck started up down the street and peeled out with a loud roar.

Chapter 10

Allie's evening wasn't going the way she had planned. She always hated when someone didn't show up for work, causing others to take up the slack, especially with a full Friday night crowd. Losing one of their regular girls had left her and Jessica to tend the bar and waitress, leaving them both exhausted at the end of night.

Allie and Jessica had worked together for six months now, and had established a closing routine.

"I've got the trash if you can finish up the dishes?" Allie asked Jessica.

"Sure thing. I'm about done restocking." Jessica wiped her hand across her forehead to stop the sweat from running down her face. Placing the trash by the door for Stan to carry out later, Allie went back to the bar and emptied all of the tip jars.

"Here's your half, Jessica. We made out pretty good for a Friday night."

"I know, but if it had been any busier, we would be dead by now. I hope they get us some help before next week." Jessica rinsed the glasses and placed them on the counter to air dry.

"Yeah, they called Trudy and her daughter to help out for the next week or two until we can get a few girls trained." Allie laid the two piles of money beside each other so Jessica could count it.

"Hey, don't wait for me, girl. I have to talk to the boss about a night off next month since we're so short-handed. I want to make sure it's on the schedule. I trust you, so take your half." Jessica waved Allie's protests away. "Shoo."

"If you say so. Thanks, I'm exhausted. Later girl." Picking up her half of the tips, Allie walked over to where Stan was waiting to escort her to her car.

No one noticed the undercover car across the street, since everyone leaving the bar was focused on getting home.

Allie had parked with the driver's side facing the bar, but was still unsure if someone might have tampered with her car. So she crouched down to look under the car, just in case.

Seeing nothing unusual, Allie checked the back seat to make sure it was empty and unlocked the door.

"Thanks, Stan." Allie climbed in, not hearing the back-passenger door open. A figure climbed into the back seat and shut the door, in sync with Allie as she got in and shut it.

Starting the car, she pulled out of her parking spot, about to drive toward the exit.

Suddenly, she was grabbed from behind by two hands holding a cord around her neck. Allie's breath was cut off and she struggled to think, *How are you supposed to hurt an attacker when they're behind you?*

All of the different self-defense techniques flashed through her mind as the attacker pulled harder.

There's only one way to stop the attack, and that is to catch the attacker off guard. Hitting the dumpster shouldn't kill us, but should give me a chance to get out, Allie thought as she started to lose consciousness.

Barely coherent, she sped up and slammed on the brakes, loosening the grip of her attacker. Throwing the car quickly into reverse, she sped up and gained momentum as she pushed the gas pedal down. Spotting the dumpster, she had a split second to aim for it. Upon impact, the attacker was thrown back into the seat and upward into the car's rear windshield. He slid back down into the seat, groaning in pain. He almost didn't notice the two men making their way over to help Allie.

Jumping out the back door, the assailant grabbed his ribs and tried running toward the place where his vehicle was parked. His injuries were making it difficult to get away from the scene, but he did and sped away.

"Hey, Allie! Wake up!" Fingers snapped in front of her face as she moaned and tried to open her eyes.

"Where did the guy go?" Allie jerked up from the seat, placing herself firmly into Justin's embrace. Looking over her shoulder and into the back seat, Allie groaned in pain from her neck moving too quickly.

Stan was outside her car, calling 911. She hadn't been out long.

"Where's Julie? He shouldn't have gotten past her." Allie became frantic about her friend. She tried to push past Justin, even though the pain threatened to overwhelm her.

Pulling back, Justin moved to let her out, hoping she wasn't hurt. Allie tried to bolt from the car, only to collapse when her knees gave way.

Justin caught her, helping her to stand up straight. "Where is she parked?"

Glancing across the street, all Justin could see was an older car with the door open. There was no sign of any type of police vehicle.

Looking at Allie, who was in no condition to cross the street, he said, "Stay here, and I'll go check on her." Justin leaned Allie against the car and took off with Stan on his heels as he ran across the street.

The woman was lying in the seat with blood oozing from her side.

He felt for a pulse, but it was faint. It looked like she'd been lying there for a while.

Taking off his shirt, Justin quickly tried to stop the bleeding, hoping the ambulance would make it in time.

Allie had regained her equilibrium and slowly crossed the street to where Justin was working to save Julie.

"Is she okay?' Allie couldn't see inside the car, but Justin was leaning over her, pressing a shirt to her side. Stan was on the phone, telling them to send another ambulance to the scene.

Justin looked up and shrugged at Allie's question. "I'm not sure. It looks like she was stabbed."

She was still breathing, so he continued to press the shirt into the wound to slow the bleeding. Blood hadn't soaked through the shirt yet, so hopefully, that meant she wasn't bleeding as badly as he had originally thought.

They heard the sirens coming closer; help would be there soon. At this time of the morning, there wasn't much action in town, so the officers arrived quickly. The squad car arrived at the same time as the EMTs. They both raced to get Julie out of the car and to the hospital.

Allie was certain the sheriff and police chief would show up since they'd been expecting Mike to come out of hiding at some point.

The EMTs were anxious to get Allie in the second ambulance, but the officers were intent on getting her statement.

"Look, I was in an accident. Someone tried to choke me to death and I crashed my car. The guy jumped out the back, and all I remember is this guy," she pointed at Justin, "and Stan calling 911. I remembered Julie, and they ran over to check on her."

"Thank you, ma'am. If we need anything else, we'll follow up with you at the hospital." The officer nodded his head at the EMTs to allow them access to Allie.

Looking over at her car, Allie realized she needed her backpack before heading to the hospital. "I need my…" Her voice trailed off as Justin brought it to her.

"I thought you might need this." Handing Allie the bag, Justin thought it couldn't hurt to ask. "Do you want me to come with you?"

"Thank you. That's very nice of you, but I just want to see how Julie's doing. We'll be fine." Allie climbed into the ambulance, ready to join Julie at the hospital.

Allowing them to look her over, the EMS declared her stable, but made her wear a neck brace to the hospital.

"You'll have some bruising, and will be sore for a couple of days. We'll take some X-rays to make sure nothing's broken or fractured."

Arriving at the hospital, Allie had to go through all the protocols to make sure she wasn't seriously injured.

"You may have a scar where the attacker tried to choke you, or it may fade with time. No concussion, so you're free to go. Although, if you wanted to stay for the night, just to be safe, we can admit you," the doctor informed her.

"No, thanks. I've been around this place more than I really want to."

An hour later, Allie was released and went to find out if Julie was out of surgery.

"Nurse, can you give me an update on how Julie's doing?" Allie inquired.

"All I can tell you is that she's still in surgery, and they're hopeful she'll come out just fine. The next few hours will tell us if they can repair any damage the knife may have caused." The nurse knew of Allie's situation, but could only tell her so much since she wasn't family.

"Do you still have my cell phone number?" Allie knew things could get misplaced in such a busy place.

"Yes, ma'am. Or you could check back later for an update. It'll be several hours, though." The nurse motioned toward the family waiting room. "You can wait in there until she's out of surgery and in recovery. By the way, there's a man out there waiting for you, and I have to say, he is *hot*."

"Hmm. Guess I'll go see who it is and why he's here. Thank you." Allie started walking down the hallway toward the emergency waiting room.

"Holding up the wall?" Allie queried.

Looking up to see it was Allie speaking to him, Justin straightened up. "Oh, yeah. It's a tough job, but someone has to do it." He extended his hand. "Hi, I'm Justin."

Taking the offered hand, Allie introduced herself. "I'm Allie. Have you heard how Julie's doing?"

Justin shook his head. "They wouldn't tell me anything since I'm not a relative. I was hoping you would be able to find out more about what was going on."

"She's still in surgery, and won't be out for a couple more hours. Thank you for taking good care of her when I wasn't able to." Allie tried to give him a way out so he didn't feel obligated to hang around.

"Did I miss something? Are you and Julie together?" Justin sensed Allie was trying to put up a wall so he couldn't get close to her. He was really hoping they weren't a couple, because he really wanted to see what other layers were hidden under this very intriguing, unique lady.

Allie was surprised at his question. "Oh, no. We aren't a couple. We're both involved in a stressful situation, and have gotten to be good friends. I like men, but I'm not really looking for a relationship right now. There's too much going on in my life that makes it complicated for me to get involved with someone at the moment."

Allie wanted to let him down easy so he didn't get the wrong idea about her. She wasn't looking for someone that felt they needed to rescue her.

Justin laughed. Karma was not being nice to him today. Helping rescue someone evidently didn't undo his rejection of Stephanie earlier.

"I know your car's not going to be drivable anytime in the near future. Stan mentioned he would get a friend to tow it over to a garage until you can get the insurance claim going." Seeing her start to protest, Justin interrupted any objections she might have voiced by continuing. "Listen, I won't ask you out on a date in the near future, but I know we both could use a hot meal after that adrenaline rush." Holding his hands out in a calming gesture, Justin hoped she would take him up on his offer. Especially considering she didn't have another option available at the moment.

"No strings attached. I can give you a ride to go pick up something to eat, then bring you back here to check in on Julie. What do you say?" Crossing his fingers, Justin waited.

"I guess that would be all right. I'm starving, and the snack machines won't work because I've tried that before. Especially selection F5. The granola bars have been in there quite a while." Smiling at him, Allie started walking toward the door, unsure of what his reaction to her accepting his offer would be.

"Let's go then. My truck's just outside." Justin walked ahead to open the door. "My truck's this way, and friends it is, for now."

Relieved he had taken her at her word about dating for the moment, Allie was thankful since she had no way to get food or go home.

Justin's truck was a fairly new Chevy that was used as a work truck, if the amount of mud on the tires was any indication, suggesting to Allie that he was guy who liked his toys, but kept them practical for work use as well.

Opening the truck door for Allie, Justin was surprised to get a dirty look from her.

"Thanks for being a gentleman and opening the door, but how in the hell do you get into this thing? Jump?" Allie was looking for a way to get up into the seat two feet from the ground.

"Here, throw your backpack up, then swing up, just like you would to get on a horse," Justin explained, but he was thinking he would have no objections to lifting her into the truck.

"Dude, hello. Not everyone has ridden a horse, so that's just as foreign to me as climbing into your truck." Figuring a little sass might cover up their awkward situation, Allie threw her backpack inside.

She was surprised as she was lifted into the air. Allie didn't have time to protest as Justin's hand cupped her rear to give her the needed boost into the truck.

"Well, in that case, I'll show you how to climb into a truck when I get in, and you can try to jump in by yourself next time." Justin grinned, because he had been able to place his hands on her rear without getting slapped in the face. He quickly hid his grin and went around to the driver's side of his truck.

"This is how you get in a truck. Place your left foot on the sideboard and bounce up while holding the handles. It should give you the momentum you need to put your other foot on the floorboard and scoot into the seat." He looked over at Allie and continued. "If you ever have to get on a horse, you have now been properly schooled."

Justin shut his door and started the truck, heading toward Whataburger, which was the only place open at this time of night. Thankfully, they'd missed the drunken crowd rush that always comes after the last call.

"Just so you know, I'll manage to get into your truck all by myself next time. There'll be no need for your assistance," Allie proclaimed with embarrassment as she realized he had firmly cupped her back end to assist her.

"Oh, and for the record, a lady never *scoots* in somewhere. We simply glide into place," Allie smirked at Justin as he tried not to laugh.

~~~

Justin turned off the truck and made it around to the passenger side door in time to open it for Allie. Still hurting from her accident, Justin managed to play the gentleman until they reached the counter.

"Go ahead. I need to figure out what I want." Allie motioned for Justin to proceed her. Before he could pay, she placed her order and handed the guy a twenty and stuck her tongue out at him. "Ha! I beat you at something this time."

"I can't let you do that, especially since we aren't on a date. I should be paying for my food at the very least," Justin protested. He'd never had a woman pay for his meal before.

"Consider it cab fare." Allie didn't want to hurt his pride, but liked to pay her own way.

He held up his hands. "I give up." Justin took his drink and went over to a booth and sat down. Allie followed, putting her backpack on the seat next to her.

"So, Allie. What's the situation you're involved in? It seems to be very stressful, and just a little bit dangerous." Justin had been certain it was normal girl trouble, and felt his jaw drop as Allie began to explain the events of the preceding week.

Allie paused when the waiter dropped off their food.

Watching the waiter carry the tray away and out of earshot, Justin questioned Allie. "So what happened tonight wasn't just some random event, huh?" He couldn't even begin to imagine what she had been going through.

"Well, we're assuming Mike is responsible for attacking Julie and trying to strangle me." Allie shivered at the thought of how close Mike had come to ending her life.

"He also tried to strangle Megan in the hospital. It seems to be his MO. He just wants the person he's hurting to be as defenseless as possible. We just aren't sure what he's trying to accomplish at this point."

"This is horrible. How could he do this kind thing to his family?" Justin was appalled that anyone would think of abusing their family.

"After trying to kill Megan, and with the attacks tonight, he should know there's simply no way he'll get Megan or Sally back. He's been a cop forever. You'd think he'd know how this works, right?"

Justin nodded in agreement.

"He does have a lot of friends here willing to take him in, but it's just a matter of time before they find him. He'll lose some of his informants when they hear what he did to Julie tonight. Especially if he continues to escalate the attacks. I'm not sure any of us have much time left before this comes to an unhappy end." Allie suddenly realized she was dominating the conversation, and only talking about a psychotic guy while there was a hot guy sitting across from her.

Apologizing, Allie hurried to explain her viewpoint. "I'm sorry. I'm sure you're not interested in hearing all this. It's just been so consuming this week, and now I've gotten deeply involved. Sally and Megan have become the family I never had."

Justin leaned across the table and grabbed one of Allie's hands. "Never take what you've been through as something to be pushed aside or ignored. You've been a huge part of making sure Sally is safe while Megan is recovering. Most people would have dropped Megan off at the hospital and left to go back to their daily lives. Very few people would've gone back to see how they were doing. You dropped everything to take care of them and put your life in danger without asking for anything in return. You're amazing. If you need anything, I don't mind helping out."

Seeing Allie's embarrassment, Justin let go of her hand. "So, what is it you do for a day job that allows you to take the week off whenever you want to?" Justin tried to steer the conversation onto a different topic.

"Don't laugh, but I'm a Nova Lady." Allie crinkled her nose at him. "For real, 'Ding Dong, Nova Calling.' And when you open the door, it should be me or one of my girls standing on the other side, waiting to take care of your beauty needs."

She held up her hand to stop any questions. "Do you really make money at that? The answer is yes, I do. When you work and follow up with your customers, they tend to become loyal customers, returning for all their beauty, clothing, and household needs. Or, as is the case of this week, protection from an abusive husband. Now that I've answered your unspoken questions, what do you do for a living?" Allie was more than curious what a great guy like Justin actually did for a living.

"I work for my parents out on their property. Kind of a handyman of sorts. I'm always around, so I think I'm kind of handy."

Unprepared for the snort of laughter from Allie, Justin was glad his comment had made her laugh, until he realized why she was laughing.

"Ah. I do have my own place, so they don't have me hanging around all the time." Justin grinned.

"Speaking of which, don't we need to get you home so you can get some sleep?"

Justin looked at his watch and realized if they didn't leave soon, they would meet the early risers coming in for breakfast.

"Oh, no. I didn't mean to keep you out all night. If it's not too much trouble, I want to go back to the hospital and check on Julie. I'll just sleep up there in one of the chairs."

Allie hopped up and took her trash over to the trash bins, assuming Justin was following her flight from the booth.

Barely catching up with her in time to unlock the truck door, Justin watched as she followed his instructions and made it into the truck on the first try.

"I'm a quick learner. I should have no problem riding a horse," Allie smirked.

"I can see that," Justin remarked as he shut the door.

Having gotten a second wind, Allie was nervous about being with Justin any longer, because he was simply wonderful.

~~~

Allie was amazed that Julie was not only awake, but coherent. Straight from surgery, Julie looked terrible, but at least she was alive.

Her face was pale, and she looked exhausted. The attacker hadn't hit anything major when he slid the knife into her side. So other than blood loss and light duty for a few months while she healed, Julie would all right.

"Hey, Allie. I'm glad that you're okay." Julie grimaced as she tried to get comfortable. "It took forty stitches to sew up the stab wound. Looks like Mike wanted to hurt me pretty bad. The doctor said it could have killed me if my rib hadn't stopped the knife's upward motion. Another inch and it would have hit my heart, causing me to bleed out immediately."

Allie was relieved Julie was still alive. "I'm so glad you're going to recover." She took Julie's hand and patted it gently. They had grown closer than she realized over the past few days together.

"Do they think Mike did it? I couldn't see who was behind me or anything. All I saw was a ski mask in the side mirror."

"I was just sitting there when he yanked the door open and shoved the knife into my side. I had no way to defend myself. I think he was certain that by the time anyone figured out I was incapacitated, I would be dead."

"We're so glad we found you before he could accomplish the job."

"I slapped at his face when he stabbed me, and then he hit me with the butt of his gun. I think he would've continued stabbing me, but something distracted him." Julie was exhausted, and it was starting to show as she gritted her teeth, trying to tell Allie what had happened.

"Who was the guy that fixed me up? The nurses said he was cute." Even in pain, Julie was still trying to play matchmaker.

Humoring her, Allie figured a little information wouldn't hurt, especially about the guy who saved her life.

"Well, his name is Justin, and he was at the bar all night. Stan was telling him to go home when I got attacked, and they both ran to help. I'm not sure what he thinks is going to happen between us now that the danger has passed. He's out there, waiting for me to tell him you're all right." Allie shrugged, frowning at the thought of how little she really knew about Justin.

"Girl, you had better get out there and let him know I'm just fine. If for some crazy reason you decide you don't want him, tell the nurses, and he can come in so I can have him for myself." Julie grinned at Allie.

"I know of the Greenley family. He's really good looking," Julie informed her. "Justin isn't known to date many girls in a serious way.

Allie just rolled her eyes at Julie. "I think the drugs they have you on have gone to your head, girl. He is good looking, but with all that's going on, I'm not sure what kind of relationship would work getting started like this. I'm going to tell him to go home. I still have the phone you gave me, and the nurses are going to call if you need anything." Squeezing Julie's hand, Allie left and went back to find Justin holding up the wall again.

"I thought the wall would've collapsed by now. I don't think you're putting your back into your work to make sure it stays up correctly." Allie smiled at him. She always joked when she was uncomfortable, but so far, Justin didn't make her feel awkward.

"It's a tough job, and someone's got to do it, so I volunteered. Can I please give you a ride? There's no way you'll get enough rest sleeping in one of these chairs." Holding out his hand, he hoped she wouldn't leave him hanging.

Taking a leap of faith, Allie placed her hand in his. "Yes, you can take me home. Just don't make a big deal out of it, okay?"

"Yes, ma'am," Justin drawled. "So she's okay?"

"Oh, yeah." Holding Justin's hand had flustered her. "Sorry. She's doing fine. You saved her life by stopping the bleeding. Thank you." Allie's unease at holding his hand lessened when they didn't see anyone on the way back to Justin's truck.

~~~

Allie fell asleep, not realizing where Justin had taken her until the truck had stopped.

As Justin parked in front of an unfamiliar apartment building, Allie began to protest, confused. "Justin, this isn't my apartment complex. I live across town."

"Your right, it's my apartment. Allie, before you say anything, let me explain, and if you don't like it, I'll drive over to your apartment." Justin held his breath, waiting to see if she was going to protest.

"I don't expect anything from you, but you've been through too much over the past week and need to rest without having to worry if someone is going to kill you. I'll sleep on the couch and be a perfect gentleman. I even own a gun, and my home security system is very good. Nothing is going to get past me to harm you. It's just for now, okay?"

Allie sat there in silence, realizing how tired she really was from everything.

"Okay. I'll stay tonight." Justin was shocked when she agreed. She simply got out of the truck with her backpack.

Walking around the truck, she waited on him to recover from her quick answer.

Joining her at the front, he pressed the button to lock it. Turning to Allie, he put a comforting arm around her sagging shoulders, guiding her toward his apartment.

Leaning her against the wall, he joked while he unlocked his door. "I guess it's your turn to hold up a wall." Smiling at her to cheer her up, he saw the sheer willpower it was taking to simply stay on her feet.

Allie was surprised when he scooped her up and carried her inside, stopping to close and lock the door after them. He continued to the bedroom, placing her gently on the bed.

Without speaking, he pulled the covers down and removed her shoes, laying them on the floor by the bed.

Suddenly nervous, Justin stood there, looking at Allie.

"What?" Allie didn't mean to be abrupt, but wasn't used to others taking care of her.

"Yeah. The restroom is right here if you need it before you go to sleep." Justin pointed to the doorway near the bed.

Placing a hand on his arm, Allie nodded, appreciating his thoughtfulness and desire to take care of her needs. "If you'll make sure I don't fall over on the way there and back, that would be wonderful."

After an uneventful trip to the bathroom, Allie managed to sit back down on the bed without falling over.

Justin took her shoulders and gently laid her down and pulled up the covers to tuck her in. He walked over to turn off the bathroom light, when Allie sat back up.

"Don't turn off the light, please? I won't be able to go to sleep for fear Mike is lurking in the shadows." Allie couldn't help the way her body started shaking, just from the idea of what Mike could do if she let her guard down.

Justin walked back over to the bed and wrapped his arms around her. "Do you want me to sleep on the floor in here with the door closed? I can even move the dresser in front of it if that'll make you feel safer."

Justin knew she was going to have nightmares for a while, but with the way she was shaking, it might take a few years before they went away completely.

"Thanks for trying to comfort me. I really didn't mean to drag you into all this. I'm usually much more independent than this. I don't understand what's wrong with me tonight."

Allie wanted to move back from Justin and his embrace, but when she thought about how safe she felt in his arms, she snuggled a little closer.

"I guess for now, I wouldn't mind if you were holding me until I fell asleep. It would be nice for someone else to worry about me for a change."

Justin smiled. "I think you need to let me take control and watch over you so you can actually rest. I'm going to go and set the alarm and make sure everything's locked up. I'll put the cedar chest in front of the door when I come back, then I'll hold you for as long as it takes for you to fall to sleep." Justin just wished he could be there to hold her for more than one night, but he would take what he could get.

Allie waited, listening to Justin as he set the alarm and moved the cedar chest. When he returned to the bed, she followed his movements as he took out a pair of shorts and headed into the bathroom.

She tried not to gasp when he came out of the bathroom in his shorts, but no shirt. Allie was impressed by his chest.

"Last chance to change your mind. I can sleep on the floor if you'd prefer." As he waited by the bed, he was certain now Allie couldn't take her eyes off his chest, so she wouldn't change her mind.

"Um, no. Not changing my mind, but it's just for tonight. No guarantees on any future sleepovers." Allie tried to say it sternly as she motioned him into bed, bringing him only inches away from her.

"Lay down, Allie. I'll be a perfect gentleman…for tonight at least. Now tomorrow, all bets are off." Justin eased her back onto the pillows and pulled her head back toward his shoulder.

Allie didn't need directions. She just snuggled into the spot next to him as she realized he not only made her feel safe, but special.

Before she could fully enjoy the touch of his smooth chest against her back, she was asleep.

It took Justin a little while longer, but he knew even without having sex, this was a woman he wanted to keep in his life. One evening of terror had given them something weeks of dating could not accomplish; an intimacy that couldn't be ignored.

Justin didn't remember drifting off, but he woke up midafternoon to the sound of his phone ringing.

Justin hopped up to answer the phone before it could wake Allie. She mumbled something and snuggled deeper into the covers, but didn't wake up.

Justin answered with, "Hey, hold on a sec."

Walking over to the door, he pulled it shut behind him as he entered the living room. "Okay, Mom. What's up?" He took a seat on the edge of the couch as he heard the beginning words of a lecture that could take a while.

"What do you mean, what's up? We've been calling you all morning. I've even texted you several times with no response. If you hadn't answered this time, your father was going to come over there to make sure you were all right." His mom pause long enough so that Justin could get a word into the conversation.

"I'm sorry, Mom. I was asleep." Justin felt awkward sitting in his boxers while his mother was on the phone, and a girl was asleep in his bedroom.

"Well, we were worried, and it's close to three in the afternoon. We've been trying to reach you since eight this morning. When we saw the news about what had happened last night at Texas Teas, we assumed if you were there, you'd be sleeping in this morning, but since you still hadn't answered, we thought you might be one of the ones who were hurt. You know how worried I get when things happen in the world and I can't get a hold of my children."

When she finally stopped for a breath of air, Justin knew his mother was waiting for answer, but he wasn't sure what he could tell her without digging a hole for himself.

Before he could comment, she started badgering him again. "They haven't released the details on what happened last night at the bar. Were you there? Did you see the girl that was attacked?"

Justin groaned. Now that his mother knew he was alive, she wanted a rundown on everything that went on so she would know if the rumors were true.

"I'm okay, and I'm sorry I made you worry. I was there, and did see most of what happened, but I really can't tell you about it since it's an ongoing police investigation. They asked us not to talk about it just yet." Justin ran his hand through his shaggy brown hair with a sigh.

"I hadn't thought about the fact they would put it on the news, but I guess it makes sense in our small town. I should have called, but it was a crazy night. We realized sleep would be the best idea since it was so late, and your call was what finally woke me up."

Ignoring his apology, his mother immediately picked up on the fact that he had used the word 'we.'

"So we're not as important as some girl after all. You do have someone over there, and you were so tangled up that you couldn't call to let us know you were okay. I guess I didn't raise you as well as I thought I did...."

"Whoa, Mom. Slow down and hold on for just a minute. It was much different than that. I wound up at the hospital with a girl, and she—"

"Justin, you better not have gotten some girl pregnant. I just couldn't take that from you, my baby. What did I teach you all those years? Now you've gone and thrown it all out the window."

"Mother, SHUT UP!" Justin yelled, shocking her into silence. "I had to take Allie to the hospital because she was one of the one's attacked. When they released her, I wasn't going to let her go home to an empty house since I knew it really shook her up. I got her some food, then offered to let her sleep here so she could feel safe and get the rest she needed. I think everything that's happened finally hit her, and she was scared. I slept on top of the covers and she slept under. I didn't want to leave her alone. But we didn't tangle any sheets, as that was the last thing on our minds. I was simply caught up and didn't even think to call you since it was almost five in the morning when we got here."

"Oh, my. Justin, I can be there in just a few minutes so I can help you take care of her."

Knowing his mother would do just that, Justin had to stop her before the entire town was on his doorstep, leading Mike straight to them.

"I really appreciate that, Mom, but no one can know where she's staying. Her attacker is still out there and has no idea she's here. I didn't even notify the police where she was since it was a spur of the moment decision." Justin decided that a compromise would the best for everyone.

"How about this. After church is over tomorrow, if she's up to it, I'll bring her out to the ranch so she can tell you the whole story. I think for tonight, if she continues to sleep, it'll be the best medicine for her. But I'll let her know you offered to come help take care of her."

Justin seriously hoped his mother would stay out of it until Allie was up and moving around before meeting the inquisition squad at his family's house.

His mother took the hint. "I'll leave things alone, only for tonight, though. I'll start something for lunch tomorrow. I'm guessing I couldn't get you to bring her to church in the morning?"

Hope would always spring eternal in his mother's plans. "Not possible, since she's kind of in hiding. Also, you know how women can be sometimes, and while lots of love is great, in this case, I think it would be a bit overwhelming for her. Let's just take everything one step at a time for now. I'll call you as we head out there tomorrow, okay?"

"Well, if you're sure you don't need me tonight?"

Justin responded patiently with, "I love you, Mom. Bye." Hanging up, he looked down and realized that a shower was next on the list of things he needed to do. Knowing that eating something would help Allie's recovery, after his shower, he would fix them something to eat.

~~~

Allie woke up to the smell of something wonderful cooking.

She groaned as she tried to stand, her muscles screaming about the abuse from the accident. Walking slowly to accommodate her bruised body, she peeked out to make sure it was only Justin in the kitchen.

"Hey, that smells amazing. What is it?" Allie was impressed he was cooking something on the stove instead of zapping something in the microwave as most single people do.

"Hi, sleepy head. That wonderful smell is the homemade chicken soup I'm making for you. I had my brother pick up the ingredients and bring them over." Justin turned from stirring the soup to face Allie.

"What time is it?" Allie felt off balance since she had slept the morning away.

Stirring the soup and replacing the lid, Justin grinned. "About nine in the evening, so you've been asleep most of the day. I would say about sixteen hours so far; although, I'm willing to bet that if you eat, shower, and go back to bed, you would be asleep again in no time. You had a really bad night."

"Oh, crap. Megan and Sally will be worried about what happened to me. They were expecting me this morning. Where's my cell phone?" Frantically trying to grab her backpack from the floor near the front door, Allie had to hold onto the counter to keep from falling over.

Justin hurried around the counter and brought the backpack to Allie, placing it on the barstool.

"Here you go." Justin watched Allie worriedly. She looked slightly green around the edges from the quick movement. He hoped she would take his suggestion, "Do you want to take one of those pills the doctor gave you?"

Taking a several deep breaths, Allie tried to regain her balance. "No. Let me call Megan, then I'll see if eating something will help. I'm not sure I could take a shower right now. I'll take a pill before I crawl back into bed, unless you're going to take me back to my house?"

Allie really hoped he wasn't going to kick her out. She'd never felt so awful before; if this was anything like what Megan had felt like last week, Allie now had a lot more empathy for her.

Justin smiled and shook his head no, then went back to the kitchen to start serving the soup. Trying not to eavesdrop, he didn't really have a choice since the kitchen was only divided from the living room by an island. Since Allie was sitting on a barstool for her call, he could hear to the entire conversation with Megan.

"Megan, I'm fine. Is everything okay with you and Sally? Oh, so you know what happened last night? Is Julie still all right?" Allie paused and let out a sigh of relief at Megan's answer.

"Yes. I heard through Karen that Julie's recovering nicely." Megan was quick to assure her.

"Thank goodness. I just woke up and realized I was out of the loop. Whew, I was worried. Even though we saw her after the surgery, I was scared something might have happened. We know how quickly things can change. They wanted me to stay overnight, but I wanted a real bed, so I left."

As Megan began to admonish her about the dangers of staying by herself, Allie interrupted her.

"After we checked in on Julie, Justin wouldn't let me go back to my apartment so I stayed at his condo. I only woke up a few seconds ago, which is why I wasn't able to visit like I promised. I'm calling to check in with you." Carefully nodding her head in response to Megan, Allie glanced at Justin.

"I would say so, but you'll have to tell me what you think in person. Is Sally really disappointed I didn't come over today? Oh, you told her I had to stay away so Mike wouldn't follow me? I agree, she doesn't need to know the whole story about what happened. Uh, Justin who?"

Motioning to Justin, Allie mouthed, "What's your last name?"

Justin realized he hadn't introduced himself properly, so he walked over and took the phone from her.

"Hey, Megan, I'm Justin Greenley. I promise to take good care of Allie, but she was hurt herself so I need to make sure she eats something and get her back into bed. No, ma'am. There'll be no funny business going on in this house, which is exactly what I told my momma. Yes, ma'am." Justin was pulling out the extra southern charm just for Megan.

"Speaking of my mother, she would be ecstatic if you could come to lunch tomorrow."

"But we don't know you or your family, and it would be difficult with our situation," Megan protested.

"I know it might be difficult, but she would love to have you and Sally join us."

"Is your mother Georgia? I've seen her around town, and we don't want to cause any trouble for anyone. I don't want to put her out." Megan knew how much work it was to have unexpected visitors, and didn't think Justin understood what an imposition it would be.

"Yes, my mother is Georgia Greenley. It'll be no trouble at all since we have company for Sunday lunch most of the time. It would be wonderful for Sally to be somewhere safe, where Mike wasn't able to look for you. I think my mother would really like to have you over for lunch, and Allie would feel much better knowing you're all right as well. Please, say yes? Perfect. I'll text you the address so you can let the officers know where to take you. We should be there about twelve thirty. Wonderful. I'll let her know. 'Night."

Justin hung up the phone and sent a text to Megan so they could make it out to the ranch.

Mouth hanging open, Allie was upset that he had a whole conversation without consulting her. He hadn't even let her say goodbye.

"So I have no say in how my life is going to be?" Allie crossed her arms angrily, waiting for an explanation as she gingerly moved to the couch.

"My mother called while we were asleep, and the only way I could keep her from showing up here was to promise to bring you out to the ranch for lunch. She would've liked to take care of you herself, but I let her know the best thing was for you to rest tonight. Since I couldn't wake you up to ask you, I just said yes."

Justin walked back to the kitchen and retrieved two bowls from the cabinet. He placed a steaming bowl of soup in front of Allie and he apologized. "I'm sorry if you feel like I took over, but I was just trying to help."

Allie felt her anger disappear as he took care of her needs. No one had ever cared enough to really take care of her, or to make decisions for her before.

"I'm sorry. I shouldn't have griped at you. So much is going on, and I feel like I'm losing control. When that happens, I tend to snap at those around me." Looking sheepish, Allie took the spoon and started eating her soup as a distraction to keep herself from bursting into tears.

"Oh my goodness, you can cook! Oh, that didn't come out the way I meant it to." Allie stopped and quietly said, "I'm shutting up now. Thank you."

Justin put his bowl of soup down and took the seat next to her.

"It's all right. You're not the first person to be surprised at my culinary skills. My mother didn't have a girl, and since I was the youngest of four boys, she made me help her in the kitchen. I can cook if the need arises. Now eat. We can work the rest out later."

Chapter 11

J.D. received a phone call around 2 in the morning. Wondering what on earth could be going on, he listened to the voice on the other end explaining what had happened at the Triple Teas Bar.

He got dressed while he listened to the voice give instructions on how to deal with the aftermath. He then grabbed his gun and badge.

"I'll be there in ten minutes." As he was hanging up, his wife mumbled something incoherent.

"I've got to go into work. Something happened, and it's all hands on deck for the time being. I might have to work on my day off, but I'll try to let you know a little later, once things have gotten under control." His wife groaned in acknowledgement and rolled over, her snores starting again.

He quietly left the house and took his truck, just in case he had to hit the country roads where his squad car would be more noticeable than just a plain truck.

Winding through the back roads, he managed to make it to the site in less than seven minutes. Looking around, he finally spotted the other truck with the front end wrapped around a tree and the door standing open, but it looked like no one was inside.

Hearing a groan, he ran over and found Mike almost passed out across the seat. He headed back to his truck and took out a blanket. Laying it across the seat, he pulled up as close to Mike's truck as he could. Leaving it running, he went around to open the passenger door and moved him over to his truck.

Once settled, Mike was still unconscious, so J.D. took Mike's wrecked truck and pulled it over to the edge of the abandoned mill buildings with his truck since Mike hadn't been able to make it under the enclosure. He covered the truck with a tarp and tried to camouflage it by leaning old boards and tires against it, to make it seem like it had been there for ages.

Satisfied with his efforts, he jumped back in his truck. The nearest town with a hospital was over two hours away. He just hoped his friend could hang on long enough to make it. He had to make sure they had a big enough population to hide Mike. Since the town of Rockwall had three hospitals, it seemed like the most logical choice.

Listening to the radio while all the chaos continued on in the search for Mike, J.D. wondered exactly what kind of trouble Mike had gotten himself into this time.

He was aware of some of the confusion from earlier in the night, and had heard 'officer down' come across dispatch while he was transferring Mike to his truck. Mike couldn't have been involved with the officer getting hurt, not if his plan had played out like it was supposed to.

Finally pulling up to the emergency room doors with a screech, J.D. hopped out of the truck, yelling and waving his arms to get the attention of the attendants inside.

"Help! I got a man that was in an accident. He's hurt really bad." J.D. made it around the truck and opened Mike's door, catching him as he almost fell out.

The nurse on duty ran out to see what was going on. "Sir, what happened?" Noticing the blood covering Mike's clothes as J.D. tried to hold him in the vehicle, she ran back inside.

"We need a stretcher. You two," She motioned to the interns standing at the counter, "come help move him. We need all the hands available."

J.D. just stood there, waiting for them to help get Mike inside. As the interns brought the stretcher out, the nurse took J.D.'s place.

"I've got this, sir. Okay, guys, grab his legs and let's move him. Sophie, help me support his shoulders and neck. Count of three… one… two… three—lift."

J.D. followed along behind them until he was stopped at the edge of the emergency doors.

"No one can come back here, sir. I'll send someone out to get the details from you in just a moment. If you could move your truck out of the way, in case another emergency arrives, we would appreciate it." The nurse didn't wait to see if J.D. followed her instructions. She continued through the doors and out of sight.

Parking his truck in the lot, J.D. returned to give the intern a statement about Mike's injuries.

"I was driving along and saw this truck out on HWY 276 with the door standing open, and this guy was lying in the seat unconscious. I didn't have any signal on my cell to call for help, so I moved him over to my truck. I'm not sure what's wrong or what happened to him, but he looks like he's been in an accident."

"Sir, did you see anything that could tell us who he is?" The intern was entering the information onto an iPad.

"Oh, there was a letter with the name Bubba Box on it." He made up a name on the spot so they wouldn't look too closely into Mike's real identity. "Is he going to be okay?"

"So far, he's alive, and the doctors here are really great, so all we can do right now is hope for the best." The intern started to walk away, but J.D. stopped him by putting a hand on his arm.

"I'll leave you my cell number in case he wakes up or needs to know where his vehicle is." J.D. left the number for a prepaid phone they were using so it couldn't be traced back to him.

"Thank you." J.D. turned and left, heading back to Roseville where they were frantically looking for Mike. He was certain if he showed his badge at the hospital, they would allow him to check on Mike when he had a chance. Considering the mess Mike had left behind, it might be awhile before he was able to take a day off and get away from town without arousing suspicion.

~~~

Allie woke up refreshed from a sound sleep to find it was only eight in the morning. When she finished having dinner the night before, she'd taken a shower, hoping the hot water would relax her sore muscles. Borrowing shorts and a T-shirt from Justin, she took a pain pill and went straight to sleep. Justin was still sleeping, so she crept quietly out to the living room and turned on the TV to watch the news.

The local news was reporting a failed robbery attempt instead of the truth about an ex-police officer wanted for attempted murder. Understanding the need for secrecy, Allie didn't want Mike to get credit for his horrible deeds, but Julie had almost died.

Suddenly hungry, Allie decided to raid Justin's cabinets and see what would work for breakfast.

Finding a box of Lucky Charms and a bowl, she returned to the living room. To occupy her time until Justin woke up, she decided to watch a movie.

When Justin woke up and rolled over to find Allie gone, he raced out to the living room, worried that she had left. He breathed a sigh of relief when he saw she was on the couch, asleep, not even watching the movie that was playing.

Hoping to make as little noise as possible, he decided to go take shower, letting her rest some more before they headed out to his parents.

Leaning against the closed bathroom door, Justin wondered what had happened to him in less than twenty-four hours. He had gone from turning down several offers for dates and serious relationships, to acting like was a married man caring for a hurt spouse. Unsure if what he was feeling was from all the excitement and adrenaline, or this feeling of affection could be something that would last, he shrugged, unable to determine which was real.

He'd heard of love at first sight, but he wasn't sure if he really believed in it. He was certainly willing to give it a try if Allie turned out to be as amazing as she appeared to be.

Being her protector was good for his male ego. Justin wasn't about to lose the opportunity to take care of her and show her that people could be nice and caring to each other.

Justin had the impression that Allie didn't have very many people who had loved and cared for her in the past. She just needed someone to love her, and it sounded like a good idea to him.

Grinning to himself, as if he'd just solved all the problems of the world, or at least Allie's, Justin started whistling while he shaved and showered. He was ready to show Allie what love from a real man looked like.

~~~

"Do you have anything I could wear since I don't have any extra clothes with me?" Allie was embarrassed to ask, but didn't want to meet his family in the clothes she had worked in the day before.

"Sure. I have a T-shirt you can wear, and there should be a pair of pants that would fit you. Just help yourself to anything in the closet." Justin didn't want to cause Allie any embarrassment, so he figured she would be more comfortable picking something out rather than him looking over her shoulder.

Allie tried on a few things, and found a pair of jeans in the back of the closet that fit with the legs rolled up to accommodate for their height difference. Justin had plenty of T-shirts, so Allie chose one with a college logo that was slightly bigger. Feeling like a voyeur as she opened his dresser drawers, hoping for some boxers that would fit, Allie was pleased to find all his stuff neatly folded. Picking out a pair with a superhero logo, Allie was thankful she had washed her bra out the night before so it could dry while she slept.

Feeling completely out of her element, she was certain that Justin's family would be so different from her foster families.

She was awestruck as they pulled into the driveway, heading toward a huge two story white house with a wrap-around porch. It reminded her of Scarlett's home from the movie *Gone with the Wind*. She hoped that Justin's mother wasn't a self-centered southern lady. She wasn't sure she could handle that kind of drama in her life at the moment.

Completely nervous about the type of family that could live in such a nice home, Allie was filled with dread as she worried about the clothes she was wearing.

She hid behind Justin as they were greeted by a pack of dogs excitedly racing up to them. Seeing Allie's fear, Justin greeted them. "Hey, doggies. Good dogs. If you hold out your hand so they can sniff it, they won't be as likely to bark or jump on you."

"I'll just stay back here and let you do the loving. I'm not really comfortable with dogs, at least not outside dogs." Smiling apologetically, Allie stayed as close to Justin as she could without touching him.

"Mom and Dad are still at church, but I can show you around until they get here." Walking toward the porch, he opened the green front door, allowing her to proceed him inside.

Allie was amazed. She expected it to feel cold, but it had a cozy, homey atmosphere that was really welcoming. She was curious to know more about the woman who had raised a gentleman like Justin, and also created a home that was warm and inviting. While there was a definite acknowledgement of their wealth, it wasn't flaunted in the furnishings. Some of the furniture was well used, and definitely not saved for special occasions. This type of home was unlike anything Allie had ever seen.

The grand tour showed a house fit for entertaining large parties, with a large dining room used for fancy dinners and lots of bedrooms for guests to stay in.

Allie followed Justin into a modernized kitchen that had all of the latest accessories, while still maintaining the history in keeping with the rest of the house.

He opened the oven to check on lunch, and a savory aroma met them.

"Makes you hungry, huh?" Justin grinned at the look of desire that filled Allie's face.

He turned on the lower oven and placed the rolls in to start cooking, while he turned the upper oven to warm so the meat didn't dry out.

"Not used to homemade cooking, are you? Where have you been hiding all these years? A microwave convent?"

"What?" Allie's attention was returned to Justin from the amazing kitchen that was distracting her. "A microwave convent? Where do you come up with these ideas? I was raised in several foster homes over the years, and most dinners were barely edible." Trying to shrug off her past, she closed the oven and caught his hand to pull him out of the kitchen.

"I need to see what else this house has in it. Lead on, tour guide."

There was a business office next to the kitchen, and further down the hallway, a modern media room filled with DVDs and wall-to-wall shelves, overflowing with books. They continued to the basement, but Allie couldn't keep the voice in her head quiet.

"Oh no, the basement," Allie teased. "Are you hiding any bodies down here?" She was aware there wasn't anyone to hear her screams if he really wanted to hurt her. Surprised to feel completely comfortable with Justin, she said, "Lead on, but you need to protect me just in case one of the bodies turned into a zombie."

"Nope. No bodies down there today." Justin was thrilled as Allie placed her hand on his arm and moved closer to him.

"Dad moved them last night since he knew you would take a tour of our house. He thought dead bodies in the basement might make you uncomfortable." Winking at Allie, Justin opened the door and headed toward a carpeted room that opened up into a large game room, with a hall leading off to one side.

"We didn't have basements like this where I'm from. They're dark and damp, with lots of laundry and spiders."

Shuddering at the memories, Allie explored the hallway and found two bedrooms, a bathroom, and a small kitchenette, making this the ideal place for an adult child to never leave the nest.

Hearing the dogs barking, she announced, "I think your parents are here." Allie nervously started up the stairs.

"'Hey, hold on. What's wrong?" Justin could tell that Allie was uncomfortable with meeting his parents.

"It's just…well, what if they don't like me? I mean, you've only known me for a few days, if sleeping is even considered as knowing someone, and I look like this." Allie gestured to her casual clothes.

"Don't worry, I'm wearing the same thing. They'll love you." Justin stopped himself from saying anything more.

Placing a comforting arm around Allie's shoulder, they made their way upstairs to greet his parents. The kitchen porch door opened as Justin and Allie made it down the hallway.

"Hello? Justin, we're home. Did you check on lunch, honey?" Georgia called out as she walked through the door.

At five foot, four inches tall, with short brown hair, she looked lovely in her Sunday suit and matching hat.

"Yes, Mom. The roast is done, so I turned it down and put the rolls in to start baking." Giving Georgia a hug, Justin turned with an arm around his mother's waist so he could introduce her to Allie.

"Mom, this is Allie Foster. Allie, this is my mother, Georgia Greenley."

"Hello, Mrs. Greenley." Allie held out her hand, but was taken by surprise when Georgia grabbed her and pulled her into a hug.

"Don't you dare call me Mrs. Greenley. I'm GG to my friends."

Hearing the porch door open, GG didn't let go of Allie, but kept her arm around her shoulders as she turned to introduce the tall, handsome man that walked through the door. "This is my husband, James. James, this is Justin's friend, Allie."

GG was so warm and friendly that Allie forgot her fear of being judged and began to relax.

Allie focused on the twin picture James and Justin made as they stood next to each other. The main difference between them was the distinguished dash of gray in James' hair.

As they broke the embrace, Allie noticed that Justin was a leaner, more toned version of his father. *MmMmm, his dad is still good looking. If Justin ages as well as his father has, I could see myself growing old with him.*

Unaware of Allie's thoughts, GG continued talking. "Justin, why don't you and Allie go set the table while I get out of these church clothes and into something more comfortable." Starting for the stairs, GG stopped when Justin cleared his throat.

"Mom? I sort of invited a few more people to join us than you were expecting. They're friends of Allie's that needed to get out of the city for the day. It should be at least three more than you'd planned." Justin nervously waited for his mother's reaction.

"That's no problem. You know I always cook enough to feed an army. Just put out enough plates for eight, and if it's too many, then we can clear them off when we're done." GG didn't seem phased in the least by Justin's announcement.

Just as Allie and Justin finished setting the table, the dogs started barking again, signaling the arrival of Megan and Sally.

Allie let out the breath of air she'd been holding. The feeling she had at seeing the both of them was unusual for her. She'd never had people she genuinely cared about before, and it was a nice feeling.

Megan was looking better since she'd had a few more days of rest. Sally raced out of the car and threw herself into Allie's arms.

"I was sooo worried, but then Mom told me you were hanging out with a handsome guy." Sally gave Justin an appraising look. "I guess he's kind of cute."

Sally disengaged herself from Allie and walked straight up to Justin. "Dude, do you hit women?" Sally looked at him in all seriousness.

Justin understood Sally had no idea most men would never lay a hand on a woman, so he got down on her level to answer her question.

"Sally, I have never hit or hurt a woman or girl before. I hope you can help me take good care of Allie while you're taking such good care of your mom. Does that sound like a deal to you?"

Sally turned toward Allie. "Well, taking care of my mom is hard work since my daddy hurt her, so I guess I can let you take care of Allie. But I'm warning you, mister, you better not hurt my Allie." Sally finished her threat by shaking her finger in Justin's face.

Seeing Megan join her daughter on the steps, Justin introduced himself. "Hi, Megan. I'm Justin. I hope I've passed the inspection."

Trying not to laugh or be embarrassed by what Sally had said, she took Justin's offered hand.

"I'm with Sally. If you're protecting our Allie, then you're okay in our book." Smiling at her daughter, she gave her a nod of approval.

Karen came forward and gave Justin a quick hug while asking, "Hey, Justin, how's it going?"

Seeing Allie's confused expression, Justin hurried to explain. "Karen and my brother used to date back in high school." Turning toward Karen, he asked, "So, I guess you're the bodyguard for these lovely ladies?"

"You guessed correctly." Spotting GG through the screen door, Karen opened it as she greeted her. "Hi, Mrs. G. Hope you don't mind the extra guests for lunch?"

Karen had been to many events at Justin's house, and was prepared for the greeting hug that seemed to be required when someone arrived at this lovely home.

Having heard most of what Sally had to say, GG greeted Megan with a gentle, welcoming hug.

"Well, let's not stand out here on the porch when the food is ready to eat. I cooked enough for an army, Karen, so you don't have to worry about that big appetite of yours going hungry." Winking, GG held the door open. "There's plenty to go around."

Seeing Sally hang back as they entered the house, GG bent down. "Do you like macaroni and cheese, Sally?" Having a few grandchildren already, GG knew the way to a child's heart was through her stomach.

"Yes, ma'am, I do," Sally whispered, suddenly feeling shy.

"Well then, you can help me carry it to the table from the kitchen, okay?" Seeing Sally nod, GG led the way to the kitchen with everyone following her.

Chapter 12

Seated at the table, everyone was startled when Megan's lawyer Mark walked in and kissed GG on the cheek before seating himself at the table.

"Sorry I'm late, Aunt GG I had to run by the police station after church, and it took longer than I thought it would." Sitting in the empty place next to Megan, across from Justin, Mark made himself at home.

"No worries, dear. We were just fixing to ask the blessing." Looking to James at the head of the table, GG took the hands of those closest to her.

Allie and Megan tried to focus on the blessing, but were too busy exchanging glances, stunned that Mark and Justin were related.

"Amen. Now, let's eat."

Still stunned and slightly confused, GG answered their unasked question. "Mark is our nephew. He comes to lunch most Sundays, and has lived with us since his mother died when he was young."

Focusing her motherly gaze on Mark, she admonished, "Any type of business you have going on can wait until after dessert, and when we don't have little ears in the room to overhear whatever is going on with all of you."

Contritely, Mark agreed, and they spent the rest of the meal catching up on the ranch happenings from the past week.

"Please, let us help with the dishes?" Allie asked, wanting to contribute and not feel like a burden to the Greenley's.

"I think if everyone grabs something and brings it to the kitchen, we can have this cleaned up pretty quickly." GG stacked the plates as she spoke to her family at the table.

"I can help as well." Megan held up her only working arm. "I've got the salt and pepper shakers." She smiled. Even though her effort to help was small, she was enjoying herself.

With everyone helping, it didn't take long to clear the table and start the dishwasher.

"Now we can go sit in the living room and discuss this situation." GG led the way to the family parlor.

"Sally, do you want me to show you how to work the video games downstairs?" Justin held out a hand to her, waiting for her to take him up on his offer.

When he returned, he sat next to Allie on the couch, placing his arm behind her. Mark was sitting next to Megan on the loveseat, leaving Karen to sit on the other side of Allie.

The parents sat in recliners, which were their permanent seats next to each other.

"So, what in the world is going on? I have never met two more innocent and law-abiding citizens than these ladies, and now they have both been attacked. Who could possibly want to hurt them?" James quietly demanded of the young people sitting in front of him.

While he normally stayed in the background, James understood more than people thought. His B.A. in Psychology allowed him to hear all sides of an argument before giving those involved his opinion.

"Would you mind explaining it all to them?" Megan asked imploringly of Allie, uncomfortable with the details.

Allie told the story with Mark's help, since some of the legal details were confidential.

Mark unconsciously placed his hand on Megan's arm to comfort her as the story progressed through the second attack.

"We spent most of the last week in a hotel, but we need to move again since the attack last night was directed at Julie and I. Mike has a way of finding out confidential information." Allie sighed at the thought of several more weeks of gypsy style living.

Justin and Mark weren't surprised when GG spoke up. "Ladies, we have a secure apartment downstairs, and Mike has no reason to suspect that you're staying with us. We haven't met or socialized with either of you before, so there's no reason for Mike to make the connection that you're staying here. You shouldn't drag Sally around anymore than you absolutely have to. We have more ranch hands around here with guns and dogs to alert us than any hotel security can provide you.

"Plus, I need someone to fuss over, and you girls would give me a good excuse to do that. What do you say?" GG leaned forward expectantly. Not many people refused her when she had an idea.

Both Allie and Megan looked to Karen, waiting for her to validate if it was a safe course of action for them.

"I'll say yes, but only if they still want us after they hear what Mike did to Allie and Julie." Karen made the decision, taking their safety into her own hands. "I have no intention of telling the local police or sheriff's office about this change of address. It'll stay a secret. The less they know about where we're staying, the better.

"We're certain there's someone on the inside feeding Mike information on our protection detail. While we expected this to happen, it's taking much longer to find him than we thought." Karen shook her head in frustration. "He stays one step ahead of us." She was feeling more comfortable with her decision as they discussed the situation.

"Mike grew up out on Lake Tawakoni and is very familiar with the area, which helps his cause, not ours. It's possible he's hiding out in a deserted cabin, or simply camping in a tent, making it easy for the officers who are canvassing the area to miss or overlook him." Karen leaned forward, showing her enthusiasm, and excitedly shared her thoughts.

"Considering Mike knew Allie's work schedule after almost a week off work is not good. He managed to slip by the surveillance we had in place, which seems to indicate a close friend on the inside is feeding him information." Nodding to Allie, who knew more about this part of the story, Karen settled back into the couch to listen.

"I was working when I met Justin. He was hanging out with some friends. He tried flirting with me all evening until we closed." Allie gave Justin an apologetic smile.

"Wait, she turned you down, cuz? I didn't think that was a possibility anymore since you'd toned up your man boobs." Mark dodged the throw pillow Justin sent in his direction.

"Hey, dude, watch the face." Justin rolled his eyes at Mark.

"Will you boys behave so we can hear the story?" Karen admonished them, as everyone chimed in with their agreements.

Allie resumed her narration. "Justin left, and we finished closing the bar. I got Stan to walk me to my car, and I guess when I unlocked it, that was when Mike climbed into the back seat. I didn't think to look a second time after making sure it was safe to get in. I turned to tell Stan good night when we saw Justin by the door, holding up the wall. Stan went to talk to him, and I got in and started the car.

"I drove forward and slammed on the breaks, which made him hit the back of my seat and loosen his hold. Then, I threw the car in reverse and put my foot on the gas, slamming hard into a dumpster. That's all I remember."

"That's terrible, but the hospital said you're okay, right?'" GG couldn't help but worry that Allie wasn't sharing the full extent of her injuries.

"I'm mostly bruised, and have to work out the soreness," Allie said. "It'll take a few days to get back to normal."

Justin took over the story. "We raced over, but we couldn't see who was leaving the car because he was dressed in black. Allie was hurt, so we focused on her. When she came to, she mentioned Julie, and we hurried over to check on her."

"Julie would have been the first person to my car if she'd seen what was going on, which meant Mike did something to her before trying to hurt me," Allie insisted. "Stan called the police and stayed with me as I walked over to where her car was sitting."

Justin shuddered at the memory of Julie's almost lifeless body. "The door was open, and Julie's body was just lying there, covered in blood. I was able to stop the bleeding, but they still had to do surgery on her to fix the internal damage from the stab wound."

Karen reached over and gave Justin a hug as Mark spoke up. "We're so thankful that you were able to help both of them. I knew Mike was an angry husband, but I had no idea he would become this violent."

"Justin followed us to the hospital, while Stan closed up and answered the police officer's questions. I was going to find a phone and find someone to pick me up when I saw Justin holding up another wall at the hospital with my backpack." Smiling fondly at Justin, Allie was thankful all of that was behind her.

"He offered to take me to get something to eat while Julie was in surgery, and then he took me to his house to recover afterward. I must have slept close to twenty-four hours, because I wasn't coherent for much of the past day."

Looking at Megan, she said, "I was relieved I didn't have to stay at the hospital. Out of fear that Mike may follow us, there was no way Justin could drive me to the hotel where you guys are staying. I really hope he was hurt when I crashed the car. I know that's a terrible thing to wish on someone." Allie started crying. "I don't know what's wrong with me. I never cry."

GG got up from her seat and came across the room, motioning for Justin to move. She scooped Allie into her arms and let her cry. "I think the rest of y'all should go into the kitchen and get dessert served. Allie and I will join you in a few minutes."

Seeing that Justin was going to stay when the others left, GG shooed him from the room as well with a wave of her hand. "You too, Justin. Out." He reluctantly left the room, but didn't go far.

Focusing her attention back on Allie, GG patted her back. "It's gonna be okay, Allie. Sometimes, you just need a good cry to get out all those pent-up feelings."

Ten minutes later, Justin stuck his head back in to check on them. Allie was no longer sobbing, but she was curled up, fast asleep. His mother nodded for him to take her place as he crossed the room, returning to Allie.

"I'll carry her to the guest room. As tired as she's been, she might just sleep all night." Justin lifted Allie into his arms without waking her.

GG walked ahead of him to open the door to the first-floor guest room and pulled down the covers. Justin placed her on the bed and covered her up with a light blanket since the air conditioning was on.

As he waited to make sure she was still asleep, he checked the room to make sure it was safe.

The windows were locked, and there was nothing in the room that someone could hide behind. He left the door partially open so he wouldn't wake her up later when he checked in on her.

He rejoined the group, just as GG was telling a story about how her older son, Luke's daughter Violet, had gotten hurt.

"You should have seen her. She was so quiet and was obviously crying when she came into the room. I couldn't see what was wrong with her, so I sat her on my lap and asked, "Did you run into something?" She shook her head no. Then I asked, "Did someone throw something at you?" Again with a no, so I asked, "Did you fall?" She shook her head no again. I was about to shake her myself when I got an idea for a crazy question. "Did you hit yourself?" Jackpot!

"Looking up at me through her tears, she shrugged her shoulders and started smiling. "I was carrying a rock with my feet and it fell on my nose." Only way I can see that happening is if she was on her back, and the rock was on the bottoms of her feet, with her legs sticking straight up. The rock had fallen between her feet, hitting her in the nose." GG finished with laughter.

It was nice to laugh over the antics of a seven-year-old, instead of worrying about the real world. Megan was enjoying herself, and Justin hoped that both Megan and Allie would be able to recover from their terrible experiences, without leaving too many scars.

Chapter 13

Sally followed the sound of laughter and found the group of adults in the kitchen. Unsure what they were doing that was so funny, Sally approached cautiously, practicing her father's rule to be seen and not heard. She thought it was nice to see her mom take a few minutes to escape her worrying and smile for a little while. After quietly assessing the scene and deciding it was safe to enter the kitchen, she hopped over to Justin.

"Hey, can we go see the horse you have out in the barn? I haven't been close to one before, and it would be sooo nice to ride one." Sally pushed out her bottom lip, just a little bit, to add to her cuteness value.

"I think we can arrange a tour of the barns for you, Sally. We won't be able to ride today, but if you get to stay here, we can start some lessons for you. Maybe your mom and Karen would like to come out there with us?" Mark purposefully included Megan and Karen so that Justin could stay inside with Allie.

"Yeah, I think a walk outside would be good for all of us. We've been cooped up for days. I need a few sunrays to get my vitamin D count up. Let's go, gang." Karen moved in the direction of the back door.

That was all the persuading it took for Sally to jump on the opportunity.

Mark held his arm out to Megan and escorted her in a slower fashion out toward the barn housing the horses.

Justin was ambushed with questions about Allie from his parents.

"Well, son, it seems like you and Allie have gotten close pretty quickly, but do you see this lasting when everything is over with this situation?" James figured he could ask one question before his wife got started with the interrogation.

"You know, Dad, I've dated lots of girls before, but not very many of them have turned me down. Most can't wait to go on a date with me so they can boast that they've been out with one of the Greenley boys. Not only did she have no idea who I was, but she isn't interested in that type of thing. She's hardworking and honest. I don't know any women that would give up their time to help someone in Megan's situation. It's extraordinary. I was almost convinced there weren't any women out there who weren't completely superficial. I could become very serious about this one if she wants me. You don't think it's happening too fast between us?" Justin stopped talking and realized that both his parents were staring at him.

His dad recovered quickly. "I knew I loved your mother when I saw her at Uncle Andrew's wedding rehearsal. Since I was walking her down the aisle, I introduced myself, and by the end of the weekend, I had a date planned. After the first date, we just knew we were meant to be together, and she's stuck with me through thick and thin. Just because it hasn't been very long, doesn't mean you can't be in love with her, right?"

Justin hadn't expected the idea of love to be brought up. "I'm not sure if I would use that word, but I do like her lot, and I really appreciate that you're going to let them stay here while things are so dangerous."

"I think I speak for both your mother and I, since you've robbed her of speech, that it's about time you got serious with a girl that has some sense in her head." James gave GG a loving smile.

"I believe us old people will go and take a nap while you check in on Allie. I'm certain Megan and Sally will be just fine with Mark and Karen to watch over them. Who knows where it will lead?" Steering GG toward their room, James left the young people to mingle without their interference.

~~~

Megan walked slowly out to the barns with Karen to see the horses. Mark was quickly pulled ahead by an impatient Sally.

"How are you feeling this afternoon?" Karen asked, holding Megan's elbow to keep her balanced.

"I'm pretty good, as long as I don't laugh too hard. It's nice to be outside after being all cooped up this week. The cast is starting to itch, but I can work with that when I see Sally happy and enjoying herself."

Taking advantage of Karen's listening ears while Sally was occupied, Megan found a hay bale in the shade to take a break and sit on.

"I'm so amazed that these people would care about us when no one ever cared when Mike was hurting me. There were times when I was with Mike in the beginning when I would just scream and hope someone would hear and rescue me. I gradually started assuming I was the freak, and that all husbands did this to their wives. No one ever came to rescue me because this was normal. I'm not sure if I can recover enough so Sally will be able to choose a different life for herself." Megan sighed with a sad smile.

"Honey, none of this is your fault. Mike should've known better than to treat his family like this. Somewhere in the process, Mike decided he would rather use his fists instead of his brains. You know the saying, you catch more flies with honey than vinegar? Well, obviously, Mike's momma forgot to explain that principle to him."

Sally ran up, interrupting their conversation. "Mom, Karen, aren't you going to come and see the horses?"

"Nope. Karen and I are going to sit here and talk about old people things. You make sure you see everything, and you can tell me tonight, okay?" Megan didn't want to overdo her day out of the hotel. Small steps to recovery for her.

"Sure thing, Mom. I'll make sure to ask Mark lots of questions so I don't miss anything." Sally started to bounce away.

"Hold on, missy. You need to call Mark by his full name, Mr. Greenley." Megan wanted Sally to be respectful of adults, and being on a first name basis was not the way for that to be accomplished.

Megan waited until Sally was out of hearing range before she responded to Karen. "I know I wasn't the reason Mike was abusive, but I feel bad that Julie and Allie have gotten hurt because of me. If I had just told Allie to go away, then this wouldn't have happened to them." Megan couldn't look at Karen as she said this.

"Allie, Julie and I have all made choices. We can't let bad things go without justice, and we can't sit around while people are killed, raped, or beaten. We have to help those who need us. I know Julie and I both took an oath to protect those in need of our help. Allie is just a precious angel that stood up for you when you couldn't do it for yourself. If you asked any one of us, we would do it all again."

Seeing Mark eyeing them as they sat outside the barn, Megan waved.

"Besides, Allie considers you and Sally family now. It says a lot about the way she feels about you both. I think you staying here is a wonderful opportunity to see how a real family operates with each other. This is one of the best families I have ever been around, so maybe a little love will rub off on y'all while you're here. Just be open to it, okay?" Karen gently touched Megan's arm so that she would look at her.

"I'm not sure I can, but I'll try for Sally's sake. This whole place just makes you want to take a deep breath and believe that everything will be all right. Is that even possible after all that's gone on lately?" Megan left Karen with the unanswered question and walked over to see why Sally was jumping up and down.

Karen smiled and looked around the peaceful surroundings, knowing this place could heal wounds. Personal experience had taught her life would go on, and the people who loved you could make all the difference in how well your spirit healed.

~~~

Getting the ladies settled in the basement apartment wasn't all that hard. Justin and Mark carried their things down in just two trips.

Megan and Sally would share one room, while Karen planned to stay in the other one. Since Allie was already asleep, Justin set her suitcase inside the door of the guest room for whenever she woke up.

Karen checked all the exits and ways someone could gain entry into the house. They had an alarm system, but they only set it when they went out of town for more than a day.

"We need to make sure and keep the front door locked, as well as any other outside doors so that no one is able to come inside when we're not aware. Plus, we need to set the alarms when everyone's in for the night." Karen wanted to make sure every possible precaution was taken to keep Mike out.

"Just remind my parents before they go to bed, since they'll be the first ones up in the morning." Justin pointed toward their room, up the stairs.

Karen sat down with Sally to explain the rules for being outdoors. "You can only go outside if one of the adults who were at lunch are with you. I don't care how much you want to go out, we need to know where you are so we can make sure you're okay. Do you understand?" Karen took Sally's nod as an agreement. "If there's an emergency, and you can't find an adult, then you need to call the police. Do you know how to do that?"

"Yes. Nine-one-one, and tell them what's happening. We went over safety rules at school. I got this, no worries." Sally held both thumbs up.

~~~

Sunday nights at the Double G Ranch were leftovers for dinner. No cooking allowed, since lunch was always a big meal.

Megan and Karen helped GG gather all the food to place on the counter, as everyone helped themselves and went to sit at the dining room table.

GG had an idea that only a Southern lady would suggest to the guests staying with her. "I think while you ladies are staying here, you should learn how to ride a horse." Smiling at Sally's enthusiasm, she got to the main reason for lessons. "I would also like all three of you—Megan, Sally, and Allie, to learn how to shoot a gun. Karen already knows, as do the ranch hands that work here."

Megan wasn't sure how they had gotten on to this topic.

"I didn't want a gun around the house with Sally, but Mike always kept his police issued gun in a lock box. I was just hoping I would never give him a reason to use it."

Sensing her comment had made everyone uncomfortable when she spoke about Mike with all of the details surrounding their problems, Megan decided to explain why it bothered her to learn to shoot a gun.

"I'm sorry, y'all. I've been trying to change my mindset from the way I have always lived. Most of the time, I'm too scared of what might happen. I didn't want to think about what he could do. He could always read my mind, and know if I was being disloyal. So when I have a thought, I have to say it out loud so I follow through with it. Do you really think Sally should learn how to shoot a gun?" Megan realized everyone was staring at her as she finished her thought.

Knowing Megan had no self-confidence, GG spoke up. "Sweetie, my children learned how to protect themselves when they were about Sally's age. We have all sorts of animals out there that could hurt them if they're not prepared. I think, considering the way things have been going lately, that it wouldn't hurt if you and Sally could kill a snake if you had to.

"Karen, do you think you could handle the target practice safely with Sally? We have plenty of guns, and there's an area out back setup for that very thing. I would feel much safer if Sally knew how to handle any guns she might come across on the ranch. The ranch hands don't leave them lying around, but accidents do happen." GG smiled like she had come up with the solution for world peace.

Everyone at the table nodded in agreement. There was no point in trying to say anything except, 'Yes, ma'am.'

~~~

Waking suddenly, Mike was confused about where he was at. It didn't look like a prison hospital, and there certainly weren't bars on the doors.

He looked around, unsure of where the hospital was located. It looked different than the colors in his hometown of Roseville, so it must be one of the bigger hospitals in one of the larger towns surrounding the area. What he couldn't remember was how he had gotten there? Had there been an accident?

Figuring the nurse would be able to enlighten him, he started looking around for the remote thingy so he could press the button. When he moved, though, pain shot through his side and all along his chest. Moaning, he stopped moving and it lessened, but it still hurt. Thankfully, the nurses were keeping a close eye on his recovery, and checking in on him every twenty minutes.

"How are you doing there, Mr. Box? Are you feeling any pain?" The nurse began to check all his vitals.

"Lady, of course I'm feeling pain. What in the hell happened to me?" Mike wasn't going to be nice, especially when he felt like a truck had run over him.

"Now watch yourself, sir. You were in an accident, and a nice man brought you in, even though he didn't have to. We aren't exactly sure what happened, but you were banged up pretty good. You were bleeding internally, so they had to go in and stitch you up. You also have several cracked ribs and a concussion. We couldn't give you a lot of pain medication until you woke up and the doctor could check on you. They were concerned because you've been unconscious for several days. Do you have any family we need to call for you?" As the nurse spoke, she methodically poked and checked every part of his body.

"No. No family. Do you know who the guy that dropped me off was? Could he come back and tell me where he found me? The details are kind of foggy to me." Mike didn't want to pass out information that would get him or J.D. locked up.

"I'll definitely call him when I'm finished examining you, but I need to know what your pain feels like on a scale of one to ten?" The nurse seemed to be in no hurry to administer the pain meds.

"Well, I would say close to a ten. I couldn't move enough to find the remote to call you with because it hurt so bad."

Mike planned to make sure that these ladies took care of him, since his own wife had obviously abandoned him. Unclear as to why Megan wasn't there to take care of him, the only thing Mike could figure out was he must have gotten hurt while undercover. Why did he feel like he was running from the law instead of enforcing it?

"We'll give you some meds through this IV, and I'll check on you in about an hour. If the pain hasn't gone away by then, we'll up the amount we're giving you in small doses. The doctor will be in to check on you shortly." The nurse finished setting the IV dispenser and left the room.

Mike closed his eyes, waiting for the doctor when the room went completely dark.

~~~

Allie was walking through a room she had never been in before when someone grabbed her from behind, cutting off all her air. She tried to scream and struggle, but her arm was pinned to her side as the stranger tightened his grip around her neck, starting to choke her. The blackness seemed to close in, but the light at the end of the room under the door beckoned. Reaching for the light, Allie woke up screaming.

Justin ran over to her and calmly tried to soothe her. "It's okay. There's no one trying to hurt you. I've got you. It'll be all right."

"Someone was in my dream, and it was so real. They were trying to stop me from making it to the light. If I had just been able to open the door, I might have seen who was attacking me."

Allie took deep breaths as it sank in that it was only a dream. A dream that made her throat sore again from someone trying to choke her screams into darkness.

Justin continued to hold and rock her gently as she relaxed into his embrace. Breathing a sigh of relief, she looked around the room.

There was a reading chair with a table and lamp next to it. The dresser had been moved closer to the door so they could scoot it in front of it in case Allie was feeling unsafe. There were two windows with a table in front of each one, and a large wardrobe took the place of a closet that looked big enough to hide someone inside. She was lying on a bed with silky, sheer blue material that covered the top of the four poster bed and draped down each side pole with silk forget-me-not flowers tied at the bottoms with ribbons to match.

This was not the room Justin had grown up in. With her awareness returning, Allie felt ashamed that she had cried herself to sleep. Justin had been sitting in the chair, reading, just in case she needed him.

"Justin, you didn't have to stay with me. I mean, I know your family is hanging out in the other room, and I don't want you to feel obligated to stay with me all the time." Allie wiggled out of his arms to look up at his face, while silently hoping he wouldn't leave.

"Allie, my family has been in bed for a while now. We got Megan, Sally, and Karen settled in the basement, and Mark went home. We have a house rule that boys and girls don't sleep in the same bed unless they're married. Mom made an exception tonight since we're not canoodling together, and it really seems to help you sleep."

Justin pulled her close again so she wouldn't try to get up. He was enjoying feeling macho and protective of a woman.

"Oh, my goodness. What will your mother think of me? I've been a terrible guest." Allie sat up again, putting her hand over her mouth in horror. "She was so nice to me, and all I've done is eat her food, cry, and fall asleep in her house. Ugh! I really loved her, though. She's so nice." Allie was ready to start crying again.

Justin laid her head on his shoulder as he spoke. "It's okay. My mom's glad she could help take care of you and Megan while you both heal. I know it's been a rough few weeks for you, and she's perfectly willing to make sure I stick around to help you out, in whatever ways that help might be needed." Justin winked at her suggestively.

Allie smirked. "Except for no canoodling, huh? Purely platonic, sleeping in the same bed with each other for weeks on end. Definitely no canoodling could happen from this situation." Justin smiled, happy that she could find humor in the situation.

"So she couldn't get you married in a normal, respectable way? Is she setting this up, hoping you'll produce a grandchild for her to spoil in the next year? Sneaky woman."

Justin started laughing as well. "I think you hit the nail on the head with that one, only she won't admit that to anyone. The rules can't be broken, or everyone would do it. This is the first, and probably only time she's bending the rules a bit to justify meddling in my future. I'm sure her matchmaking senses are all aflutter. Why didn't I see she was doing that?" Justin hit his forehead with the palm of his hand. "The rest of the family won't let her meddle in their affairs, so she decides to pick on me."

"Really, Justin, you have a wonderful family who looks out for you. It's not something everyone has in their lives. I've never had a family. Not a real one, that is." Allie wasn't looking for pity. It was just frustrating that those who did have a wonderful family always took it for granted.

"Oh, don't get me wrong, Allie. There are days when I would love to walk out that door and never speak to some of my family again. The reason I don't is because I love them too much to do that. While there will always be arguments and disagreements, that's part of what our family does; we're always there for each other. I know that's hard for most people to understand when we joke around or dis on each other, but there's not one of them I wouldn't give my life for."

"I've seen a lot of families through the years, and while many say they're a loving and caring family when it comes to sticking together, they're sadly lacking." Allie didn't want to judge others, but she had never seen a family that was this selfless.

"I think you might be right. We tend to take our family for granted when so many out there don't have more than a mom or a dad. It's just the way it's always been for us." Justin had a hard time understanding Allie's point of view because his family had always been there for him.

"I mean, look at Megan. There was no one to help keep her from Mike's abuse. Her family isn't in the picture. Once she married Mike, they weren't around. I know I sound cynical, but I haven't had many good examples of what a family really means." Allie hoped this family would be there for Megan and Sally.

"I'm sure once you stay here a few days, you'll realize this is one of the good ones. There are no take backs on the declarations of love in this household. Also, I'm pretty sure my mom has already started the adoption process to officially bring you into the family." Justin hoped when the time came, Allie could accept someone who would love her for life.

"Then this is really going to be awkward to be sleeping with my new brother. Just not sure how adopted I want to be into this family if this is the kind of behavior that goes on around here." Allie shook her finger at Justin.

"I'm not sure if I can deal with all this closeness. Let's go get something to eat. I'm starving." Allie teased him to take the focus off herself for the moment.

Chapter 14

Monday morning was an adjustment for the whole group. James and Justin went out to help with the chores in the barn, and returned in time to start helping place the breakfast dishes on the table.

Sally was helping GG cook the eggs, while Allie set the table. Karen and Megan started preparations for dinner so it would be ready that evening, without anyone spending extra time in the kitchen.

"Good morning, ladies," Mr. James greeted as he walked in and gave the cook a big kiss.

GG playfully swatted at him. "James, behave. There are children present," She chided as she gave Sally a wink.

After almost forty years of marriage, there wasn't much their children hadn't seen in the way of hugging and smooching. He blew her a kiss as he grabbed the last tray of cups and headed to the dining room.

"I think it's sweet you guys still like each other enough to flirt. It gives me hope there might be some nice men left in the world. I didn't think they existed." Allie couldn't resist looking toward Justin to see how he handled his parents' playfulness.

Megan hadn't been around anyone that displayed affection with their spouse before. Sure, in high school, there were always couples making out, but not older married people. It was supposed to stay in the bedroom, out of sight.

Karen spoke up for GG "They've been chasing each other for many years. Thank goodness, they keep it all PG rated for those of us who don't want our eyes to fall out. GG and James have stayed together by always expressing themselves, and it's always been nice to have a good example for the rest of us. Even when they fight, they always make up eventually."

There just might be a way to find love and have a lasting marriage after all. Allie felt hopeful for the first time in a long time.

~~~

After breakfast, Karen took the ladies outside for shooting practice. One of the ranch hands had brought out several different guns and setup the targets before he left for his ranch duties.

"Are you ready to try shooting?" Allie asked excitedly.

"I want to try the shotgun. It looks so cool." Sally was having a hard time not touching the guns in front of her.

"Why don't you try the BB gun first and get used to it, then I'll let you graduate to the handgun. The shotgun has a big kick to it, so only the adults need to try it. Sorry, chica." Karen began to demonstrate safety etiquette for handling a gun.

Thirty minutes, and many resetting of the targets later, Karen looked at Megan and declared, "Those two are top-notch shooters. Are you ready to see what you're made of?" she asked, hoping Megan would take the opportunity to practice.

Allie could tell that Megan was having trouble with the idea of guns. "Why don't Sally and I go ahead and get drinks ready for us to cool off with?"

"Sure, Allie. Can we make lemonade?" Sally ran over to take Allie's hand as they started back to the house.

"We can ask GG I'm sure they have something we can make that'll be refreshing." Allie glanced worriedly at Megan as they left.

"I don't really feel comfortable shooting a gun. I understand all the reasons GG gave us last night, but I just don't like the idea of possibly having to use one of those on Mike."

Karen understood her dilemma. "You still love him, don't you?"

Megan just nodded her head. She put her cast covered arm up to cover her face and started crying. "I really shouldn't love him after all he did to me. I know that up here." She tapped her head with her finger, then pointed to her heart. "It's here I can't tell what to feel." Tears were running down her face.

Karen sat next to her on the tree stump, and consolingly put an arm around Megan's shoulders.

"The thought of violence is repulsive to many people, but in this case, we know there's someone that's ready and willing to use violence against you and others you care about. Loving him explains why you were able to stay with him for so long. You can't punish yourself for loving your husband." Karen's arm went around Megan's back to help reassure her as Megan tried to wipe her tears away.

"Remember, you have Sally, and while Mike trying to kill you wasn't the best way to leave the situation, you can start over and build a new future with her. You're giving her a chance to have a different future than you were given," Karen urged, hoping Megan would give herself a chance.

"Megan, you haven't had a good role model of what love is, but you've been looking at others to show you instead of looking at what you feel inside. You're the only example Sally will care about, and you've shown her your love since the day she was born. The Greenley's may make mistakes, but they can show you how to love again as well."

Karen felt relieved to see Megan stop crying and a smile peek out. "I'll be okay, I promise."

Karen was certain Megan would take her advice to heart.

"I understand what you're saying with my head, but I don't think that I could point a gun, much less shoot one at Mike, even if that was our only option." Megan had no willpower when it came to not loving the man she had been married to for over ten years.

"While no one expects you to shoot Mike, there will always be evil people out there who we need to defend ourselves from. I haven't ever had to shoot anyone, so I can't help you if it happens. But I do know that having the knowledge of how to shoot a gun can help deter someone who might try to harm you.

"Look, I would never force you, or anyone for that matter, to go against their convictions, but I don't think convictions are the problem here." Karen didn't know what to say that would make Megan more comfortable with the situation.

"If staying at the Greenley's means that I have to shoot a gun to make everyone happy, I guess that's a simple request, considering the fact that I'm bringing danger to their doorstep." Assuming they wouldn't leave her in peace until she did, Megan stood and faced Karen. "All right. Let's get this done."

Before leaving, Sally had placed new cans up as targets. Megan determinedly walked over to the small table holding all the guns, targets, and ammo. Placing the earplugs in her ears, she gingerly picked up the shotgun, checked the gun to make sure there were shells in it, raised it to her hip and shot. She was determined to get this over with so she could move on and try to forget Mike might be the potential target.

Hitting both cans on the first try, she sat the shotgun down and picked up the handgun. Flipping the safety off, she held the gun awkwardly with her left hand trying to make sure she had a firm grip, squared up her shoulders and feet, then slowly squeezed the trigger, hitting the other target. Flipping the safety on, she laid the gun down and took out her ear plugs. Ignoring Karen's openmouthed expression, Megan walked slowly out to pick up the target cans and headed back to stand in front of a stunned Karen.

"I never said I couldn't shoot, just that I didn't want to. After all, I do live in Texas. Can we go back to the house now?"

Megan didn't mean to sound bitchy, but she was tired of being treated like she couldn't do any thinking for herself.

"Mike may have taken my self-respect and self-confidence away, but that doesn't mean I haven't lived in the world for the past thirty years. I actually knew how to do a few things before I married Mike. It's like riding a bike, somethings you never forget." Megan took the ammo and targets and laid them on the table as she headed to the house, not waiting for Karen to join her.

Karen shut her gaping mouth and smiled. Megan was a fighter. It would just take a while for it to resurface from all those years of hiding.

Around lunchtime, Justin had finished working for the day. While lunch was always a highlight in the day, he was really looking forward to seeing Allie and finding out how the shooting practice had gone.

Maybe Karen would let Allie go into town for a while, just to get out of the house.

Surprised to enter a quiet house, Justin had to search to find the one person he wanted to see the most. Waving at his mom in her office, he continued on until he found Allie in the playroom, playing a lively round of foosball with Sally.

"Allie, I'm sorry, I think you might be able to beat the kids this weekend, but no grown-ups are allowed. Thanks for helping me practice, though, because now I can show Timothy he's wrong."

"Who's Timothy? And why is Timothy wrong?" Allie was confused how a foosball game could bring enlightenment to someone.

"Well, he's one of the boys I go to school with, and he always says, "You're just a girl, and they can't do the same things boys can do, like play sports," but girls can be good at sports and games too, right, Allie?" Sally planned to make Timothy eat his words.

"Girls can win at sports, but it's not really nice to gloat when we do win. It could make the other person feel really bad about losing." Allie wanted to make sure Sally didn't take winning too far.

"Exactly! Last time he did this dance about him winning and me losing. I didn't like it at all." Sally was certain she could show him just how awesome girl power could be.

Justin couldn't wait any longer after overhearing their conversation. He knew exactly how competitive Timothy could be, because he was his nephew. Considering how competitive the grandchildren were, it was a good thing Sally had some time to practice before the weekend when the other grandchildren arrived.

"Hey, beautiful ladies." Justin included Sally, making her giggle.

"I'm not a lady, Mr. J. I'm just a beautiful child. You have to be old to be a lady." Sally took advantage of Allie's distraction of looking at Justin to score a goal.

"No fair!" Allie pouted at Sally.

"Okay. We can redo that one point because of game interference. Ugh! Men!" Sally shook her head at Justin so seriously.

"I'm going to take a shower, then we can go grab some lunch and pick up the stuff you need from the apartment. Sorry for disturbing you, my lady and child." Justin bowed to them as he backed out of the room, trying not to laugh at Sally.

Allie finished by letting Sally have the last point that broke their tie.

"Why don't you practice a while longer by yourself, because I need to run upstairs." Allie wanted a chance to hang out with Justin instead of playing more foosball.

"Sure. Justin's probably going to take you on a date. That's why most guys shower. Otherwise, they don't take one for several days. The things we put up with, right?"

"Um, he might be. I should go see what he has planned. Thanks for the heads-up." Shaking her head as she walked up the stairs, Allie had no idea how Megan dealt with a child that smart on a daily basis.

～～～

Justin and Allie headed out in Justin's truck with the promise that if they saw or heard anything unusual, they would call 911 immediately. Their first stop was to check in on Julie, and see how she was feeling.

Julie was in a secure room of her own, having been moved from ICU the day before.

Following the nurse, who checked to make sure Julie was awake before allowing them in, they saw her was sitting up.

"Well, you look about as good as I feel. I'm still sore from the other night. How are you feeling today?" Allie walked in and took a seat near Julie.

"I would be doing great if we could quit meeting at the hospital like this. I mean, really, can we find another place to hang out?" Julie tried to smile, but it came out more as a groan as she moved.

"Hey now, they feed you free food, and you don't have to share the TV with other patients. How could we resist meeting in such an awesome place?" Allie grinned.

"So, other than the awesome scenery, how are you doing? Really?" Justin didn't want to overlook the tiredness on Julie's face.

"I'm told I'm alive because this guy saved my life." She looked at Justin. "There are no amount of thank yous I can give, but I want you to know I'm so glad you were there for both Allie and I. I won't forget it."

Julie tried to lean forward to shake Justin's hand, but fell back onto the pillow, exhausted.

Leaning forward, Justin patted Julie's hand. "You just get better, and if Allie will let you, you can give me a big hug and kiss."

"I'll have to take a rain check on that for a while, I'm afraid." Julie tried to stay still so she didn't hurt as much.

Ignoring Justin's attempts to flirt with Julie, Allie asked about her stay. "So what do the doctors think about your injuries?"

"The doctors didn't think I would make it through surgery. They kept me on monitors to make sure they didn't miss something while they were stitching me up. Mike stabbed me twice, not once like they had first thought, but managed to miss any major arteries. My organs were not quite as lucky, though. A few were just nicked. They got everything stitched up, but I needed a transfusion to get me stabilized."

"Will you be able to work again? Or is your career with the police force over?" Justin was hoping Julie wouldn't have to quit her job.

"I won't be able to work again for at least six months, and possibly a year, depending on how quickly things heal. They wouldn't tell me anything except that you and Megan were okay."

Julie was glad to see some other faces, but she realized she might have taxed what little strength she had. Pressing the call button for the nurse to bring her pain medication, Julie listened to the details Allie had for her.

"So far, Mike hasn't been found. We stayed at the Greenley's house last night. Karen stayed out there with us as well, and they're going to let us stay until this is over. No more hotels and traveling for us. They've been really awesome. We're keeping our housing situation on the down low for the moment."

Allie wasn't sure how much she should tell Julie, so she tried to keep things light.

"We had target practice with guns this morning, so if Mike shows up again, we won't be defenseless."

The nurse came in, interrupting them. "I'm going to give her something that will knock her out, so you can't stay much longer." Pressing something on the IV, the nurse left as quickly as she had entered.

"Thanks for coming by, guys. Justin, it was nice to officially meet you, and please take care of her. She's a rare find these days." Julie fought to keep her eyes open as the medicine hit her system.

"We'll come see you tomorrow. Rest and get better, Julie. Bye." Allie patted her arm and headed for the door, so she missed what Justin did when he said goodbye.

Leaning in to place a kiss on Julie's cheek, he whispered, "Don't worry. I'll take care of her as long as she lets me. I've got her covered for you. Just rest."

Leaving the hospital room, Justin reached over and took Allie's hand. Allie wasn't sure what it meant, but decided she would just roll with it and see where it led.

Chapter 15

"Goodbye, faithful car. It's been an honor to use your luxurious seats and air conditioning in this Texas heat. You have done a wonderful job. Go to your salvage yard and rest. Peace out!" Allie tapped two fingers on her chest in salute.

Turning back to Justin, who was trying not to laugh, Allie lifted an eyebrow.

"Did you know that air conditioning comes standard in cars that are sold in the south? It's not even an option here." Allie was always freezing when she went inside somewhere, then roasting when she came back out.

Allie bent over to pick up the box with her belongings from her car, but Justin beat her to it. "Go, let the clerk know we have everything, and the insurance people will be out this week to look at it. I've got this." He inclined his head toward the junk yard office, where the owner was watching them closely.

Concluding her business with the man, Allie was ready to go gather her things from her apartment and head to Justin's to get some rest.

~~~

At Justin's house, they unloaded everything into the living room so Allie could sort and organize all the orders.

"I feel like we're rushing this just a little bit." Allie started sorting, trying not to waste any time.

"What do you mean? I'm just standing here watching you. You're the one fluttering around." Justin spoke from his perch on the barstool at the counter.

"It's kind of like I've moved in, and we're not even dating yet." Allie turned and gave him an exasperated look.

"I can take care of that problem. Taking you on a date, I mean. The offer's still good." Justin grinned as he realized Allie wasn't upset at the idea of moving in with him.

"We can discuss this later. Right now, I have to get my orders put together so everyone can have their stuff delivered today."

"Yes, ma'am. I'll leave you to your business. Let me know when to load stuff up again. I don't want you hurting anything by lifting more than you're ready for." Justin flopped down on the couch and turned on the TV so he wouldn't be tempted to watch Allie's every move.

Thirty minutes later, they were back in the truck, ready to deliver the Nova products.

Not as joyful as she had been the week before, Allie still chatted as she met with her customers and gave them their orders.

Dollie's Salon was on her weekly list, so they went there first to unload as many orders as possible.

Justin opted to sit in the truck while Allie went inside. He was nervous about what the ladies inside would say about a male presence in their inner sanctum.

Allie was assaulted with questions the minute she walked through the door.

"Who tried to attack you Friday night?" One lady in hair rollers turned off her hair dryer to ask questions.

Waving her hairdresser away, another lady anxiously asked, "Was there anyone in the car with you?"

"Where have you been all of this time?" Another lady called out.

Dollie spoke up. "We've been worried about you."

All Allie could hear was jumbled noise.

The room fell silent as everyone realized Allie hadn't responded to their questions.

Seeing she had their attention, she said, "I helped a friend out last week, and when I left work on Friday, someone broke into my car and tried to choke me for trying to help her." She pulled the scarf from her neck for dramatic effect.

"Oh, my goodness. Your attacker did that to you?" Dollie came over to examine it closer. "Looks like the attacker got mighty close to doing you in, dear. Someone certainly didn't want you to help your friend anymore, that's for sure."

Allie figured the best way to answer their questions was to finish the story. "There was an officer watching over things at the Triple Teas, and he attacked her as well. She was stabbed twice, and is recovering at the hospital. The police aren't sure who did this to either of us, but they're doing their best to find them."

She blushed as she explained her rescue. "It just so happens that an amazing man came to the rescue of the officer, and he took me home with him. He claims it was for my own good. I wasn't really sure about it that first day, but he's kind of growing on me." Allie waited for the knowing looks and raised eyebrows from the older ladies.

When no one spoke, Allie looked around at their expectant faces.

"Well, don't keep us waiting." The lady with rollers motioned for her to continue.

"Carry on with the story," a voice from the back of the room called out.

"We're not getting any younger, you know." A woman with tinfoil all over her head commented to the women's laughter.

"Justin was a perfect gentleman, and kept his hands to himself. He took me out for lunch with his family too."

"Who is he, honey? Is he local?"

"Yes. He's lived here forever. We may have to go out on a few dates to get to know each other because I would so adopt his family right now. Does anyone know anything about the Greenley's?"

Seeing their heads nod up and down, Allie pried further.

"I need the scoop, ladies. Don't hold out on me. Is there a serial killer in the family that I need to worry about?" Allie figured that even their perfect family had to have skeletons in the closet somewhere, and these were the ladies to know about them.

"Oh, sugar, you managed to hook the youngest Greenley. Justin, isn't it?" Ignoring the looks from the other ladies, Dollie continued. "His family is just the sweetest. There are a few crazies, just like in any family, but we love his family, don't we ladies?" She raised her eyebrow to let the others know they could now share their opinions; everyone had a story to tell Allie.

"Well, GG is all about helping others and doing charity work with her church and in the community."

"Raising that brood of boys, and every one of them are just as handsome as their daddy was in his day. Oh, I remember how cute of a couple they made."

"So what you're telling me, ladies, is that I should run out to the truck where he's waiting…" Allie trailed off as all the ladies raced to the window to peek out at him. Justin waved from the cabin of his truck, smiling, not seeming to be affected by all of the attention he was suddenly getting.

She snapped her fingers. "Ladies, hello? So do I take him home and keep him?" Allie thought their reaction was a good indication she had picked out the right guy to be rescued by.

One of the ladies who was in her early 50's answered Allie's question. "Honey, any one of us would do him in a heartbeat. All he would have to do is give the signal and we would be all over that." Her statement was followed by a chorus of uh-huh's and oh yeah's.

Now that the story was out, Allie hoped the ladies would excuse any mistakes with their orders in the coming weeks, chalking it up to lovesickness. Not that she was in love or anything, but it would be a good excuse.

Waving bye to all the ladies and promising to be back next week, Allie was glad the delivery was over with. Now that she had put her story out there, she hoped the gossip would die out quickly, and they would be onto other exciting news by the weekend.

Allie climbed into the truck and breathed out a relieved sigh. "Whew, that's done. Can we go back to the Double G Ranch now? I think I'm finished with everything I want to do for today."

Justin snickered. "Did they give you a hard time about me?"

Uncertain if she should to tell him about all the older ladies who evidently had the hots for him, she figured he should at least know how popular he was so he could defend himself.

"So all of those ladies have the hots for you, and I'm not really sure how this works. I mean, I really appreciate all you've done for me, but I blew you off to start with, and I know you could be hanging out with someone you could settle down with. I'm taking up your whole day to run my business errands, and you seem just fine with it. I don't get it. How could you want to be with someone like me? Trouble seems to follow me around, and I don't know how to make it go away. It's part of the reason I've never dated much. I don't trust other people or their motives."

Allie finally looked at Justin, who had driven straight to his apartment. He was listening, and hadn't uttered a single word since she had started her tirade. He pulled into the driveway and turned off the truck, then took her hand and leaned toward her.

"I'm not sure where all this self-doubt is coming from, but I know we've been brought together for a purpose. I've enjoyed my single years, but it's been amazing being with you the past three days. Without sex clouding up the getting to know you process, it takes some of the relationship pressure off." Justin watches Allie's face to make sure she's following his train of thought.

"Don't misunderstand, I'm a guy. I always want to do "it," but I like getting to know you. There's something about you that makes me want to know what makes you tick. I liked you when I saw you at the bar and wanted a date then, remember? So when you're ready to date or go further, just say the word. Until then, I'm going to take you in the house and go get us some dinner. Then I'll have all evening to figure out what makes you so mysterious." Justin leaned over and gave her a quick kiss on the forehead, completely friendly in nature.

He hopped out of the truck and went around to her side, opening the door and helping her out.

Allie smiled and accepted his help. As she climbed down, she landed right against his chest. She looked up when his arms went around her in a steadying motion. Having a little chemistry between them wasn't as horrible as she had imagined.

"I'll take you up on dinner, and we can get to know each other better. With all that's going on, I'm not sure I'm ready for a bedroom playmate, but I will let you know when you have a green light." Allie tried to step back, but was held tightly by Justin's arms.

"I'm really good at being patient, so don't think you can get rid of me when I've found a snoring partner with no demands." He released her and took her hand, walking side by side up to the front door.

"Why don't you think about what five things are life-changers for you, and I make a list as well and we can discuss them over dinner. How does that sound?"

Justin grinned at Allie as he opened the door and turned the alarm off.

"I mean, what if you were one of those girls who leave the toilet seat up, or squeeze from the middle of the toothpaste tube instead of from the end? Those could be deal breakers." Wiggling his eyebrows up and down at her, he tried to defuse the tension they were both feeling.

"Here behind the door is where I keep my gun, just in case you need it. I think you could use a little alone time, since you're used to having hours to be by yourself after work." Justin finished checking the house before he left.

"Thanks for being so understanding about stuff I haven't even realized yet about myself. I haven't really had much time alone this past week, and really appreciate the quiet. I'll be fine while you're gone. Besides, I have things to think about. Now go. Bye."

Shutting the door behind him, Justin chuckled to himself. "She sure is a firecracker."

~~~

Justin found himself lost in his thoughts while waiting for his order at the restaurant.

I had girls fawning over me just three days ago, and now I'm only interested in one, Allie. A committed relationship wouldn't have crossed my mind if Allie wasn't the one I wanted to be with. I always liked that I could sample all the different flavors this world had to offer, and now I'm thinking about buying the whole carton.

Allie's a flavor all her own, though. She's confident in so many ways, yet she doubts her self-worth constantly. He smiled to himself as he thought about all her attributes.

Jumping in to help her friends when they needed it without any thought for her own well-being. She's building a business by helping others as well. She really believes she can help others improve their lives, yet she closes down when I mention I want to stick around and might like her. I wonder what happened in her past to make her so skittish. I don't think she's ever had a family, or someone that loved her before. She seems to think someone is going to stab her in the back at any moment, which unfortunately could be true this week.

Justin shook his head as they called his name to pick up the food.

I never considered long-term, but after three days, I'm still intrigued. I haven't been bored yet, and we haven't really been apart. I'll just take things slowly. It's not like I have to start counting down fifty years of married bliss, but it's not as horrible as I thought.

Let's see where these next few days take us.

~~~

J.D. hadn't been able to go back to check on Mike, a.k.a. Bubba, over the weekend, but since it was Monday afternoon, he could sneak away for a few hours.

Mike was awake and in his own room when J.D. got there. If J.D. hadn't known Mike his whole life, he wouldn't have recognized him. His whole face was a massive purple bruise, and a bandage graced the top portion of his head. They had all his ribs wrapped to help them heal. J.D. realized just how close his friend had come to dying.

Mike looked up when he heard J.D. approach. His mind had been foggy since he woke up, and he wasn't sure if he was supposed to know who J.D. was or not, so he let him make the first move.

"Hey, Bubba. How are you feeling?" J.D. wasn't sure of his reception with Mike.

"I was beginning to think you left me here to rot. What took you so long, and when can I get out of here?" Mike joked at J.D.

"Well, Bubba, the doctor told me you have some serious internal issues because of your broken ribs. It tore up some of your intestines, and will take a while before you can be back on your feet. From what they told me, it looks like you can go to a rehab facility for your extended care since you don't have anyone to help you." J.D. was still trying to process Mike's condition. Hearing about his injuries was one thing, but J.D. wasn't prepared to see how weak Mike looked.

"It might be the best way to let the heat die down until you're able to finish what you started Friday night. Everyone's on alert in the county, and you would be caught before you could park the car at the moment."

"So you're just going to abandon me here to whatever the doctors want to do with me? What if they decide I need to go home? What will I do then? Why is everyone looking for me?"

J.D. wasn't sure how to respond. He didn't want to upset Mike, but he also wanted to keep his job, which would be hard to do if he continued to help Mike.

"You attacked Allie, the girl who helped your wife leave you. Then you stabbed Julie, an officer. She almost died. You don't remember?" He scratched his head, feeling unsure. Mike was always the one in charge, and J.D. didn't know what to do now.

"I thought Megan leaving me was a nightmare. You mean she actually had the gumption to do it?" Mike was amazed.

"Uh, well, you kind of beat the living snot out her, then proceeded to try and kill her while she was in the hospital. Are you saying you're proud of her for leaving you?" Bewilderment was written across J.D.'s face as he waited for the answer.

"Of course not, dummy. I'm just surprised that she would try it after all these years. I still have to make her come back, and if that means hurting those who are helping her, then so be it. I'm sorry Julie got hurt, but when you protect scum like Allie, then that's what happens. At least Julie isn't dead, but now she won't get hurt when I take back what's mine." Mike remembered everything now. It had just been pushed to the side by his pain.

"There's the Mike I know. I told the nurses to contact me when you get ready to leave. I won't abandon you, but I have to be careful because they're watching all of us. They think there's a mole in the department that's helping you. It won't help either one of us if we're both thrown in jail."

"I think I can move you this weekend while the wife goes shopping. I got us some burner phones so you can call if you think of anything you need before I get back."

Mike responded sarcastically. "Uh, clothes would be nice. I don't really see myself leaving the hospital in a gown. See if you can setup a private nurse to watch over me instead of a rehab center. I'm nowhere near old enough to be in one of those places." Unhappy about being so far from home and away from all the comforts of his hometown, Mike was starting to lose it.

"Sure, Bubba. I can work something out, but I don't have a lot of cash to get you a nurse or anything." J.D. didn't have a problem with his suggestion, he just didn't have that kind of cash on hand. Unlike Mike, J.D.'s wife balanced the checkbook since he could never figure out how it worked, and she would notice if money was missing.

Mike was silent as he contemplated the best way for J.D. to get some cash for him.

"If you go behind my house and dig up the rosebushes directly beside the shed, you'll find a bag with cash in it. It should be more than enough to get me a room at the extended stay place here in town. Plus, enough money for the nurse to have cash up front. That way, if I leave in a hurry, I don't have to worry about paying her."

"I can sneak out after my wife goes to bed and collect the money for you. The neighbors won't see anything they shouldn't," J.D. assured Mike.

"I think it should work, but you need to find a nurse from here. If I start asking around, it'll cause more trouble in town, and it needs to be someone from the city."

Patting Mike on the shoulder, J.D. turned to leave as Mike spoke. "J.D., if I find out you've betrayed me, just know I know where you and your family live and sleep. Don't think you can take my money and leave me here. Even hurt, I'll be your worst nightmare. Just a friendly warning to think about in case you had any ideas."

J.D. nodded. "That's more like the Mike I know."

He rushed out so Mike couldn't voice any other threats. Mike needed to get better, or die from complications, because if he was free, then nobody was safe from his vengeance. J.D.

knew he didn't have the guts to take Mike out himself if it came down to it.

~~~

When Justin got back with their food, Allie was relieved when he focused on eating instead of the questions he wanted to discuss.

"Should we eat at the bar, or sit at the coffee table? I'm ready to dig in" Justin was unsure which was more comfortable, since he didn't have a dining room table.

"Coffee table. I have balance issues, and I've been known to fall off a barstool before. Yes, it's really happened and no, I don't know how I do things like that. I break all the laws of physics."

Allie took the drinks from him and walked around the couch to set the cup holder in the center of the table. Sitting on the couch and sliding to the floor gave her a back with something sturdy to lean against while she ate.

Justin placed the food on the table between them, and took a seat on the floor across from her.

Allie started opening up the containers. "Yay! You got chips and salsa. I love to eat salsa, but here in Texas, it's always so hot, I can hardly eat very much of it. Sam's restaurant has the mild kind." She was hoping her rambling would keep him from asking questions.

Justin wasn't one to be deterred, yet he decided to keep it light, sensing she was nervous about a date. "So you're one of those Yankees, huh? Not from Texas originally?"

"No, I lived in New York State as a foster child. I got to see all sorts of family situations over the years. I think the longest I stayed in one home was about two years. I've moved about thirty times, adulthood included, but I've been in Texas for almost two years now, and it's kind of growing on me."

"What made you decide to come to Texas?" Justin couldn't imagine leaving everything he knew and heading to a completely different part of the country without friends or family.

"Well, you know the game you play when you're kids? Where you spin the globe and see where you land?" At Justin's nod, she continued. "I had a map and was throwing darts to see where I landed. I had no real ties up there and wanted to try something new." Allie shrugged like it wasn't a big deal to move and start over. She could never tell Justin about what happened in New York. The papers she had signed kept her from telling him why she had really moved to Texas.

"The furthest I've been from this area was when I was in college at UT in Austin. The first semester, I came home a lot, but once I got adjusted and made new friends, it was easier to stay there. By summer, I had a job there, and wasn't able to come home nearly as often."

"I'll bet GG hated that." Allie knew they had a close-knit family.

"When I stayed the summer, she contemplated renting an apartment there because I was her baby, and she didn't want to lose me. I know it was hard on her, but she decided if I was going to be any kind of normal adult, she had to cut the apron strings."

"Why didn't you just move back to the ranch after school?

"I decided it was time to move out of the nest for good and get my own place to prove I wasn't some overgrown child dependent on my parents."

"So how many times a week did GG drive over to wash your undies and clean your house for you?" Allie teased Justin about his mother hovering over him.

"Ha-ha. She did manage to come visit at least once a month so she could cook for me. I do know how to do my own laundry and take care of myself. It's part of the reason I came home, to help Dad manage the ranch. I needed a place of my own, enter the apartment. Otherwise, I would've been lovingly smothered."

"What about your family? When did you go into foster care?" Justin didn't want to pry, but he was curious.

"I wish I'd known my family, but my mom and dad were killed in a car crash when I was one. As far as they could determine, I had no relatives who wanted me, or that could take me in. So I went into the foster care system." Allie didn't want sympathy from Justin.

"I would've wanted you. What happened when you turned eighteen and had to leave your foster home?"

"At eighteen, I was put out to live on my own. I had a few scholarships because of my good grades in high school, and attended a Junior College to get my associates degree."

"Now I'm curious. What did you get your degree in?" Justin understood more about her issues with commitment each time she explained a little bit more about herself.

"It's a degree in business management. I'd planned to try and start a business eventually, but with trying to make ends meet, well, it hasn't worked out yet."

"What type of business? Automotive? Dance? A supermarket?" Justin was trying to help Allie smile.

"Ha, very funny. A supermarket? Really? No, I was thinking more along retail, or a boutique type of business venture once I found out what I thought the area really needed.

"Instead, I met Mrs. Pat at the sports store and she got me started in the Nova business. I work less now than I did, and all the sales I do, I make full commission on. It's been great to meet new people and really get to know them. I've only been selling for about two months, but I've established a routine that seems to be working. The next step is to really grow a team and train them on how to work on their business and make it successful." Now that Allie was talking about the things she was passionate about, she couldn't stop.

"I'm still not sure what exactly I want to do with my life, but since I started selling Nova, I can see all the possibilities this business holds. I mean, Nova gives women a chance to get back on their feet and realize their true self-worth. Not just what others say, but they develop confidence that lets the world see their potential. I want to be part of changing lives so women can become independent, and not rely on a man." Allie looked over to see what Justin's reaction to her comments were, only to find him laughing at her.

"What's so funny?" Allie asked, but was uncertain that she wanted to know the answer.

"Here you say you don't know what you want to do, but then you have a list with points and subpoints and everything. I think helping other women that are in situations like Megan, or even those who are looking for a way to make ends meet is a wonderful idea." He reached across the table and took Allie's hand.

"I also find the idea of an independent woman to be very sexy. Do you know where I might find one of those women around here?"

Allie just rolled her eyes. "Whatever!"

"Seriously, Allie, the idea you could support yourself apart from a relationship is not a bad thing. I know some liberated women take it too far, but when you make a commitment to each other, you should be on equal ground. By having a job, a woman is able to fulfill parts of her inner self that a spouse is just not able to provide in her life. I could tell you that you're amazing all day, but when you hear it from your colleagues and coworkers, it means more because they're trying to do the same job you're excelling at."

"Well, amazing is something that'll take a lot more work than what I'm doing now. You really don't have a problem with your girlfriend having a career, even if she might make more than you do?"

"No, silly. My ego might have a little problem adjusting, but in the long run, it means that I picked someone that I couldn't only relate to, but admire and respect. An independent woman might be able to keep up with me and keep me on my toes. I want someone I can respect, and who will respect me. If that isn't happening, then there's not a relationship; it's just sex. Those kinds of relationships don't last very long. I want the kind that last fifty plus years or death parts you from your partner. The whole enchilada. Scared yet?"

Shaking her head no, Allie sat there taking in all that he'd said. He wanted a full, long-term relationship, white picket fence and all. He didn't want a quick boink in the bedroom.

"Are you telling me you're serious about us starting that kind of relationship? Lasting fifty years?" Allie thought if she wasn't scared before, she was now.

"I'm not asking you to marry me right now, so no. I would like to see where this could go. But if you could handle hanging out with me for the next half a century, then yes. Can we give it a try?" Justin didn't want to put pressure on her, but just to plant the idea in her head so she would think about it. Don't answer now. Give it a couple of days to think about it and let's see where we stand then, okay?" He breathed a sigh of relief when she nodded.

They cleaned up after dinner and headed back to the ranch since there was safety in numbers, and it would be harder for any incidents when everyone was on alert.

That night, as Allie laid there, trying to fall asleep, listening to Justin's steady breathing, she realized they hadn't even discussed the fact that she might not need a sleeping buddy. He'd just come in and crawled into bed with her, never once saying anything to encroach on her virtue.

Smiling to herself, Allie concluded how amazing he was.

He has more self-control than most of the men I've met. He makes me feel safe. The whole idea of someone who's interested, but wanting a long-term relationship doesn't seem as crazy as it did just a few days ago. Judging from how Justin treats his mother and family, it seems there might be more to him than I thought. I always thought families like theirs didn't exist except in the movies. They're so much better than any TV show could ever portray.

Justin's willing to get to know me, even with my trust issues. If he could take care of me when there was nothing in it for him, then what would he be like once we're actually together?

I've always had to watch out for myself because there was no one else to help when things went wrong. It might take a while to let Justin in, but I think I want to if he can be patient with me. He might be worth keeping around.

Drifting off, she pondered ideas of how to let him know what she had decided.

~~~

Throughout the morning and afternoon, Allie looked for a moment to let Justin know she was willing to give a physical relationship a try. Trying to enjoy the family atmosphere, Allie was becoming increasingly nervous that she wouldn't get a chance to tell him about her change of heart until everyone left to tend to their daily duties.

"Do you want to go downstairs and shoot some pool?" Allie didn't want to be obvious, but wanted to get Justin some place where they wouldn't be disturbed.

Subtly flirting hadn't worked during the first game, so Allie was going to have to put it out there so he would make a move, literally.

"So, Justin, I know we've been sleeping together this week, and I appreciate how considerate you've been, but I'm feeling fine now."

"So you're kindly telling me it's time to move out, huh? Guess it had to happen eventually."

Shrugging his shoulders in acceptance, Justin moved to take his shot at the table.

"Oh, no. That's not what I meant. Just the opposite, in fact. I know we have chemistry, and I want to see where it leads us. We could ignore it, but then we'd always wonder what would have happened. I guess what I'm trying to say is that the ball's in your court." Allie grinned over at him, missing her shot at the eight ball because she was concentrating on Justin's reaction.

"Actually, I'm really starting to feel I have this big wart on my nose that's growing larger, and it's making you not want to kiss me. Maybe I'm wrong, but…" Allie never finished her sentence.

Justin swung her around so that she was sandwiched between the table and his body. He leaned in to kiss her thoroughly. Grinning, he relieved her of the pool cue.

"I always thought your wart was cute."

Justin didn't give her a chance to answer as his hands found her rear end. Gripping it, he nipped at her lip with his teeth before he slipped his tongue in her mouth for a sizzling kiss.

Allie's free hands made their way slowly up into his hair to tilt his head down for better access to his mouth.

He lifted her onto the pool table, sliding into the space between her legs for a perfect fit. Moving his hand up to cup her breast, he teasingly unbuttoned her shirt with the other.

Breaking their kiss to help with the problem, Allie quickly unbuttoned her shirt and reached over and yanked Justin's T-shirt over his head in an attempt to speed things up.

Justin placed his shirt with hers on the table and took Allie by surprise as he leaned her back, using the shirts as a pillow. Proceeding to kiss his way from her mouth.

Losing focus of her thoughts, Allie wrapped her legs around his back, pulling him closer.

Justin was perfectly content to leave their pants on until, he was ready, but Allie had never had someone make her tremble from a kiss.

"Oh, Justin," she moaned as he licked and kissed his way up and down her body. She grew nervous as he moved toward the button of her pants.

I hope I can do as good of job when it's my turn, she thought to herself.

They both jumped as the door opened at the top of the stairs, indicating someone was about to catch them.

Allie scrambled to adjust her bra and pull her shirt on while turning her back to the door. Justin slid his T-shirt on before Sally made it to the bottom step and could see them.

Justin ran a hand through his hair. "We'll continue this later," he promised.

Chapter 16

With no sign of Mike during the week following the incident, the officials decided to reconvene and discuss what protective measures they could keep in place for the near future.

Allie was trying to return to work at the Triple Teas this weekend, but there were some issues that needed to be addressed first.

The Chief of Police, Dan Slayer, called the meeting at the ranch to order.

"Attention, everyone. We've been looking for Mike for two, almost three full weeks now. There have been a few signs that he's still around the countryside. It looks like someone's helping him, but we haven't been able to find anything on that front either. I'm the only one who knows exactly where you're staying. While I would love to keep you out here, protected forever, we just can't use the manpower or funds to continue doing it.

"The general consensus is for us to let Allie go back to work like normal. Justin will act as her bodyguard, sitting at the bar all night and watching her surroundings. We've already spoken with your boss, who has agreed to keep you behind the bar, serving drinks, and let the others waitress this weekend. If things go okay and there are no other incidents, then we'll consider sending Karen back to her regular duties."

Megan spoke up. "Mike won't stop trying to find me. There's nothing you can do to keep him away from us, and there are a lot of other people out there that need to be protected. I don't want any more people to get hurt because of me." Karen started to speak when Megan cut her off. "Look, Karen, you've done a great job of taking care of us. While I'm not sure where Mike is, I know this is the safest place we could stay. We have lots of people looking out for us, and Mike would have to be really bold to just walk in here and take us out. It's time for us to move on and start living without him. I'll still be scared, but that's okay because I don't think it'll ever get better. So, Chief, let's try this weekend, and if nothing happens, then you can take the protection away."

The discussion moved away from Megan and on to the logistics of Allie returning to work, and what to do in case there were sightings of Mike. "We'll give Justin an emergency license to be security since he already has a concealed handgun license. Thank you for working with us."

Chief Slayer went to leave, but was stopped by Megan.

"I would like to thank everyone for trying to keep Sally and I safe during this difficult time. If Mike doesn't show up after this weekend, then we'll be moving into an apartment in town. I don't want to impose any longer, and I'm so thankful you were willing to let us stay here. It's time for us to stand on our own two feet." Megan sat down and tried not be self-conscious as everyone stared at her.

"Megan, James and I have discussed this, and we're willing to let you rent the old guest house from us, provided you're willing to clean it out and help do some repairs. Would that work for you?" GG looked at Megan, hoping she would choose someplace a little safer than living in town by herself.

"I'm going to look for a job, but I can pay you until I get back on my feet again. Are you certain we won't be in the way, though?" Megan didn't want to be a burden to anyone ever again.

"We'll be glad to have someone using that house, and it will take a little bit of work to make it livable again. We can discuss the details of money and draw up a contract later, but we've adopted you into our family, and that means watching out for you as well. We can always do a better job of that if you're closer to us. By next Monday, we can have a game plan, and ready to get you through the next year." GG had the last word as everyone left to get ready to work.

~~~

On Friday, Justin and Allie left early so they would have time to get setup. Since Allie hadn't been to work in over a week, there was plenty she needed to do to restock before the rush that evening.

"Hey, Stan, I'm here to look over the floor plan with you. How many doors lead outside?"

"We have four main exits. Here, let me show you where they are." Justin followed Stan as he pointed out the security details.

They returned after making sure all the doors were closed and locked, and Justin surveyed the room.

"Can we move these mirrors around so we can see things a little better from the bar?" Justin sat on a barstool to see which angles would work out the best.

"Yeah, we can do that, but I need to help Allie with these cases. Rearrange whatever you need to."

Justin left Stan to help Allie move some cases of beer to restock, while he made sure there wouldn't be any blind spots from where he was sitting.

"Is it okay if I start on the extra protection plan now?" Justin didn't want to get in their way.

"Sure, dude. That's more of a one-man job anyway. Knock yourself out." Stan agreed as he lifted a case of beer onto the counter.

Justin planned to install loops to hold the shotgun under the bar, so if anything happened, Allie could grab it and protect herself. The owner already had a baseball bat hidden in the gap between two cabinets behind the bar, but this would be added as extra protection.

The evening went off without a hitch. The only people present were paying customers of the Triple Teas.

Desperate not to repeat the previous week's incidents, the chief himself was waiting to escort them to Justin's truck and provide an escort to Justin's apartment.

Justin texted: We're safe, and no one's under the bed. 'Night.

Chief Slayer responded: Have a good night.

Once they were inside, Allie realized it was their first night together without interruptions since the basement.

"Um, did you know we're alone?" Allie wanted to see what Justin's response would be.

Ignoring her question, Justin finished making sure everything was locked and the alarm set before taking Allie's hand and heading for the bedroom. Knowing their time alone was limited, he wanted to reassure her of his intentions.

"Now we can finish what we started without any interruptions." Allie couldn't stop herself from giggling as he scooped her up and tossed her onto the bed.

Justin moved slowly until he captured her mouth with his, savoring the moment. He kissed away her hesitation until she was responding with all the pent-up desire they'd kept hidden, just waiting to resurface.

They began the time honored discovery of each other in which no words were needed as they started exploring their future together.

~~~

Allie woke to find herself wrapped in Justin's body, unlike previous mornings. Trying not to panic, she slid out of the bed and went to take a shower. Hoping this was not a one-time deal, and that her fears were unfounded, Allie was almost finished with her shower when Justin joined her.

Making her self-conscious in the light of day, Justin kissed her good morning, as if they weren't standing there with nothing on.

"Now I feel like the person with a wart on their nose. Did I change overnight?" Justin covered his face with his hand in an attempt to put Allie at ease.

"Nope, not anymore. I'm good." Relieved that nothing seemed to have changed between them, Allie finished her shower.

Justin had other things in mind besides getting clean, and there was nothing to stop them from exploring their new boundaries. The cold water pouring out of the shower head only changed the venue as they moved to the bedroom and continued getting to know each other better.

~~~

J.D. had promised to help Mike move out of the hospital, so he went straight to his hospital room to find out when they planned to release him.

"It's about time you showed up. I'm so ready to get out of this hellhole. The nurses don't know what the hell they're doing. It seems like they poke you with needles, and just watch the clock to come back in here and poke you again." Mike was beyond thrilled to see J.D. arrive to rescue him.

"Don't you have to wait for a doctor to release you?" J.D. had everything ready in the truck for Mike, but didn't want to take a chance that anything would go wrong when he wasn't near a doctor and medical help.

"I'm signing myself out against medical advice. I can't spend one more minute here. I'll commit murder if you don't get a wheelchair and roll me out of this joint." Mike sent a message on his phone as he waved J.D. out to find the chair.

A nurse arrived with the chair. While she was helping Mike into it, J.D. collected his meager belongings.

Once they made their way to the ground floor, J.D. asked the nurse, "Can you stay here with him while I pull the truck over?" He was certain the nurse would be ready to abandon the surly patient if not asked to stay.

"I'm going with you. I'm the nurse he hired. Don't worry, I won't ditch you, even when he lets his temper get the best of him. Go get the truck, and once he's settled, I'll get my car and follow you. Oh, I'm Suzie, by the way." She introduced herself by holding her hand out to J.D.

"Ah, nice to meet you. Now I don't have to worry as much."

"Will the two of you quit gabbing and get on with it? I want out of this place." Mike's impatience didn't seem to affect Suzie, but J.D. looked guilty.

"Sorry. Right, I'll just be a minute," he said as he hurried away.

After Suzie helped him get Mike into the truck and she went to get her vehicle, J.D. spoke. "Don't do anything to make this woman suspicious about who you really are. Just take your medicine and treat her as nicely as you can. She might not give you your meds, and you could end up in a prison cell." Knowing Mike could be unmanageable when he was upset, J.D. thought a little advice would be a good idea.

Impressed with J.D.'s authoritative attitude, Mike shot back. "Hey now, I know how to behave. I plan to work hard and be out of this miserable place as soon as possible. Hopefully, she won't have to stay full-time after this week. When will you be coming back to bring her groceries and give her a break?"

"She made an appointment for Friday to see the doctor and make sure everything is going good. I should be able to sneak away again next weekend. If the doctor thinks things are going well, I can drive you back to the cabin and set you up out there." J.D. was hoping with Mike back in town, things wouldn't be as stressful. "We're short-staffed with you gone, and the others are out babysitting your family. It makes for some long shifts. If you stay out of trouble this week, I think the chief will cancel the protective details." The pressure from work and watching out for Mike was giving J.D. stomach ulcers.

"Did you find out where they're staying?" Mike sat up straight in excitement, only to groan when the quick motion caused pain to flare through his whole body.

"Actually, only Chief Slayer knows where they are, and he isn't saying. They're meeting Monday to discuss everything, but this hospital visit has been in your favor. Since they're having trouble finding you, they're going to call off the search. I can do some checking this week, so when we get you back next week, you can find your family quickly." J.D. stopped the conversation as they arrived at the hotel and the nurse met them at the truck.

"Thanks, man. Keep checking into those details for me, would you? When I feel better, it would be nice to have a home to go to," Mike said, feeling anxious to get his family back together.

J.D. checked him into the hotel and accompanied them to the rooms. Making sure they were settled, and Mike had the duffle bag with cash, J.D. left with the promise to return as soon as possible.

~~~

The big house was bustling with energy as everyone anxiously awaited the arrival of Chief Slayer to find out if it was safe to resume their normal activities.

Allie looked around at the gathering of Megan, Mark, GG, James, Karen, and Justin as she prepared to spring her announcement on the group. Sally had been sent to the basement to play while the adults had their meeting.

"I plan on staying in town with Justin for the next several weeks. I still want to wait and see what's going to happen, but I feel more comfortable with him, and I want to get to know him a little better." Allie smiled shyly over at Justin.

"Oh my gosh. Allie, that's wonderful." Megan jumped up to hug Allie.

"I also have an announcement. I'm going to start working on the guest cottage and see what I need to do to make it livable. I think Sally can stay out of school a little longer, but I'll have to make a decision on sending her back in the next week or so." Megan wanted to return to normal, but didn't want to give Mike the chance to harm a school full of people in the process.

Everyone quieted as Chief Slayer entered the room.

"Well, we've had no sightings of Mike over the weekend, and I think it's time to cautiously move on with your lives. Be aware of your surroundings, and if for any reason you feel uncomfortable, then please call us and we'll come check it out for you." Chief Slayer hated to be the bearer of bad news, but it was part of his job. "Karen, I'm sorry, but it's time for you to return to your regular duties. I'll need those reports from you."

"I'm packed and ready to head back to work today, Chief. I'll have a report to you tomorrow when I get back to the office. If you need me for anything, just give me a call and I'll run down to help." Karen was sad to leave everyone, but was ready to get back to her regular work with more action involved.

"Awe, we'll miss you." GG had always wanted Karen for a daughter, but fate had other plans. She reached out and gave Karen a hug.

Everyone in the room followed GG's lead and hugged Karen as she headed out. Chief Slayer followed her, stopping long enough to reassure Megan. "We'll keep looking for Mike, but he's probably still focused on finding you. Be very careful, please. Call me if you need anything."

The entire family stood out on the porch as both vehicles drove away.

"Well, I guess we'll head back to town now. Allie needs to get her deliveries done. I just need more alone time so we can get to know each other better." Justin winked at his family.

"Hey, now. Just because we've been hanging out, doesn't mean I'm going to ignore work. I know what that look means, mister, and it won't work with me." Shaking her finger at Justin as they walked out to his truck, Allie was far enough away that no one could overhear their conversation.

Megan, Sally, and GG looked at each other as they were left standing on the porch.

"Well, I guess now would be a good time to check out what needs to be done before we can move into our new house. Sally, what do you say?" Megan took a deep breath, feeling overwhelmed with the days ahead, filled only with quiet and loneliness.

"Oh! Can we ride the golf cart down there, GG?" Sally jumped up and down with excitement.

"I think that can be arranged." Placing an arm around Megan's shoulder, GG said, "Don't worry. We'll get you settled, and all your friends will be back. Heaven knows we don't want to be around Allie and Justin while they make eyes at each other."

Seeing the smile return to Megan's face, GG breathed an inward sigh of relief.

~~~

The guest cottage was situated to the right of the big house, closer to the fence line near the road, but within walking distance. It looked so cozy from far away, but as they drove closer, the ladies could see it was going to take some work to fix things up.

The shrubs around the house were overgrown. The entire outside would need a paint job, and some of the boards on the sides needed to be replaced. The porch looked sound, but the steps leading up to it would have to be rebuilt so that someone didn't fall through.

Megan tried to imagine what a coat of white paint and a little yard work would do to the place. It would be a good place to heal emotionally and physically. Anxious to see the inside, she hurried around the side of the house to the front door. Thankful for concrete steps that were still sturdy, she opened the door.

Megan was hit with a cloud of dust as she walked through the opening.

Sally and GG started laughing when Megan turned to face them, covered in layers of dust and dirt.

Sally giggled. "Mommy, how many times have you been told you have to take a shower every day? This is just not acceptable, young lady."

"Watch it, missy, or I'll find some dirt to throw on you so I can wash your mouth out with soap." Megan joined their infectious laughter.

Reaching the grass at the bottom of the steps, Megan turned her head upside down and shook until most of the dirt had landed on the ground.

GG and Sally couldn't contain their laughter, even when Megan pinned them with a motherly stare. Feeling determined and more at ease, Megan marched back up the stairs, a grin flitting across her face.

This was the perfect place to start over. With only four main rooms, the inside was small and cozy. The living room had two doors—one on the left leading to the kitchen, and the other to the back room that held the door to the back porch. Taking the left to the kitchen, Megan took in the charming fifties style Formica countertops and chrome handles. Turning to the right, there was a small hallway with a closet, and on the left side was a small bathroom.

Megan continued toward the bedroom. With the thought of sharing this house with Sally, she could see the faded paint turn into vibrant blues and yellows, colors that would bring the room back to life. There wasn't a closet, but they could always find a wardrobe that would work.

The room to the right would be perfect for an office, with space for Sally's toys. Connecting back to the living room, the house had a circular design and was perfect for their needs.

Opening the back door, Megan was entranced by the view. The tree on the left side of the porch gave lots of shade, but the vines that had grown up around the banisters supporting the roof would have to go.

Megan felt a sense of peace as she stood there looking out at the other house with the barns and horse corrals beside it. The safety of having people close by if they needed help was reassuring. Megan would be able to be alone when she needed to get away from the good intentions of this amazing family.

Turning back to see what Sally and GG thought of the house, Megan was ready to get started.

Sally ran from room to room as she explored the whole house, ignoring the adult's conversation as she imagined things in her own world.

GG's practical side, as always, got down to business as soon as they'd finished looking around.

"Most of the furniture will need to be aired out and cleaned. Each room needs a new coat of paint, but you'll need some kitchen utensils and curtains for the windows. These are so flimsy, and people can see right in. We can bring the trailer over here and load anything you don't want to keep onto it, so once you're done painting, it'll be ready for you to move in to."

Megan began her lists. "Well, I guess we'll just have to go through these boxes here and see what we need to store. I'll have the guys bring us supplies and make sure they get the back steps rebuilt so we can come and go much easier."

Rolling up her sleeves, GG went to the living room. "Let's start bringing the living room furniture outside. Then we can clean and paint whatever you want to keep. I'll figure out where to store what you don't want."

GG pulled out her cell phone, and after a few calls, she had people there, helping to clean and haul what they needed out. Megan was afraid there wouldn't be any work left for her to do.

"Don't worry, dear, I can only steal the guys for a short while, and we'll need all their muscle. We'll have to do all the fun stuff, like sorting and painting. Do you like to paint, Sally?" GG assumed it was a given, but wanted to include her.

Nodding her head, Sally, who was watching all the activity, couldn't do more than nod.

Throwing up her hands, Megan gave up trying to worry. GG seemed to have it under control. "Just tell me where you want me to start."

~~~

Allie came back out to the ranch several times over the next few weeks, as Megan cleaned out the cottage. GG had been right. After the first two days, most of the cleanup fell onto Megan and Sally.

"So how's it going, Allie? I feel like it's been forever since we got to see each other for more than a minute the past few weeks." Megan was feeling lonely because Sally was about to start back to school.

"Megan, I saw you yesterday morning. I understand what you mean, though. I'm looking forward to hanging out for the next twenty-four hours while Justin goes to this auction. I have no desire to hang out with a bunch of cows." Allie was planning to have fun as they painted the last two rooms.

"We have everything moved and sorted, so when we get done painting, we can move in officially." Megan was excited at getting to start over.

"Go say goodbye to your guy, since he's leaving for a whole day." Megan thought it was cute that Justin and Allie hadn't been apart since she had moved to his apartment three weeks ago.

Kissing like they would never see each other again, Justin reluctantly left Allie standing on the porch of Megan's new home and joined his father for the drive to the auction.

"You would think I've said goodbye forever. I miss him already, and he's not even out of the driveway." Allie felt strange with the unfamiliar feelings that grew stronger as Justin's truck pulled away.

"Maybe you're in love? It would make sense for you to love him, and I know he loves you."

"How would you know that? He didn't tell you, did he?" Allie suddenly panicked. "What am I supposed to do?"

"Uh, I would suggest you tell him when he comes home. It doesn't hurt, I promise. It only hurts when they leave you." Megan realized that she'd never had the warm fuzzy feelings of love, even when she and Mike had first gotten together.

"You don't think he'll laugh at me or reject me?" Allie had never had someone who truly loved her before.

"I think all you need to do is tell him." Megan turned to go inside the house.

"If only it were that simple." Allie sighed and followed Megan, ready to get started on anything that would take her mind off of Justin for a while.

~~~

Neither woman saw the glint off the binoculars in the field that followed their movements. Patience would win the day for this tired soul. He couldn't wait for the moment when they realized he'd found them.

Chapter 17

Mike found his family living at the Double G Ranch with the Greenley family. While there seemed to be the occasional police car that drove by, he knew Karen was no longer around, providing protection for his family.

Watching the ranch from his hiding place in a field just across the road in the overgrown grass, Mike saw the ranch hands and many family members that were around to protect Megan and Sally.

It appeared that Allie was no longer staying with Megan. It seemed that she had hooked up with Justin and was staying with him in town. At least she had quit meddling with his family and moved on to other interests.

Having recovered, Mike was still not feeling in top shape, but J.D. had helped him with a makeshift tent, sleeping bag, and chair so he could sit comfortably and observe the routine of the ranch.

As he watched with growing hatred for the pain they had caused him, he thought of how Allie and Megan would pay for what they'd done to him.

Seeing Allie kiss Justin, Mike was hoping there was a way he could take all her hope away and crush any future dreams she might be contemplating. He would think of a way to get to them if there wasn't an opportunity in the near future.

He couldn't handle the fact that they were sitting in the house, all happy and cozy, while he was sitting out in the heat. They would pay for this behavior. He would make them understand what happened when the head of a family was crossed.

The activity on the ranch hadn't changed over the past several days, as Megan and Sally were escorted around when they were outside. All the ranch hands wore guns, and the amount of dogs running around would make it more difficult, but not impossible to get closer to them.

He could always drug some steaks and give them to the dogs, but he had to figure out how to distract the entire household long enough for him to get close to Megan and Sally.

Patience and careful planning would put him within reach of his goal.

He watched as several ranch hands got the trailers hooked up to two of the trucks. Taking a chance, Mike scrambled to get close enough so that he could hear where the ranch hands were going.

The guys were cleaning out the trailer and didn't notice when the bushes by the fence shook.

"Good thing the Greenley's are picking up some extra cows at the auction." Chris, the ranch hand, scraped the shovel along the bottom of the trailer so it would loosen the cow manure so they could clean it out with a broom.

"Job security is what I call the cattle auction. The drought hasn't been near as bad here as it has been further south. So it makes good business sense to buy when the cattle are cheaper and sell when the market goes up again." Harry, the other ranch hand, swept the trailer of all the loose droppings.

Mike ducked and hit the ground as they both left the trailer, walking over to the piles of hay. He needn't have worried about them seeing him, because both guys couldn't see anything over the loads of hay they were carrying to fill the now clean trailer floor.

"At least we get a trip out of town for the night. By the time the auction's over, it'll be too late to load up for the night, so we get to stay out. Nothing like getting paid to have fun."

"Justin's a pretty cool guy and pulls his own weight, but he'll drive back to be with his new woman."

"Hey, now, can't blame a man for taking advantage of a good thing." Chris winked at Harry suggestively.

Mike left while they were getting more hay for the trailer. He needed time to work out a plan to sneak in and see Megan since the women would be left at home and unprotected. The less ranch hands who were around to stop him from seeing his family, the better.

Returning to his lookout, Mike made a call to his helper in crime.

"Hey, can you bring me several steaks tomorrow around lunchtime?" Mike had a plan to get everyone focused on the other side of the ranch while he had a little chat with his family.

"Sure, buddy. Do you need anything else?" J.D wasn't certain what Mike had planned, but was willing to take a chance on Mike's family being reunited with him.

"Yes, actually. Bring five gallons of gas and matches. That should do the trick, and I might need your help with my distraction plan." Mike was excited that after weeks of recovery and waiting, it might finally be near the end.

Arriving the next day around noon, J.D. parked his personal vehicle on a seldom used side road in a cornfield. Mike met him on foot and took the steaks from him.

J.D. drove around to the back side of the Double G ranch. They got out and started pouring gasoline up and down the stretch of overgrown fields so it would spread, and the attempts to control it would take quite a while.

Hopping back into the truck, they pulled out as Mike lit several matches, throwing them out into the field. Watching the flames ignite in the side view mirror as they drove away, Mike felt satisfaction as the damage quickly grew.

"That should keep the ranch hands occupied for a while and give me time for a cozy chat. Drive back to my camp, and I'll sneak across the road with the steaks to feed to the dogs." Mike rubbed his hands in glee.

"Yes, sir. I'll park down the road and wait for the call that they need help containing the scene. Good luck." J.D. pulled to a stop and Mike hopped out to go see his family.

He arrived back at his hiding place to watch and see how long it would take for the family and the rest of the ranch hands to clear out to take care of the fire.

Once the alert was sounded, people began racing in all different directions. No one noticed when Mike walked up to the back door of the guest house, leaving a trail of drugged meat behind him for the dogs to follow and devour.

He pounded on the door, hoping the urgency of the knock would make them open up without looking to see who it was.

Allie had arrived just in time to help with the painting of the last two rooms.

"Finally, we finished the bedroom. Now for a break." Wiping her paint brush off and closing the paint can, Allie straightened. "Oh, I think I've used muscles I had no idea existed."

"Here, Sally, take these and go to the bathroom and rinse them out in the sink, please. Then we can take a break." Megan began to peel the tape off the corners and from the windowsill.

A loud pounding sounded on the back door. Megan glanced out to see vehicles and people moving around in a panic.

"Allie, something terrible happened…" Megan broke off as she realized Allie had opened the door and silence had followed.

Mike was standing just inside the room, closing the door with his foot.

Megan froze in the doorway as she saw the gun Mike had pointed at Allie's back.

"Lady, take your gun out and put it on the floor. Just know that I also have a knife with me, so if you try anything crazy, I'll gut you, just like I did Julie. Now sit over there on the floor in the corner." Mike tossed zip ties at Megan, causing her to snap out of her daze.

"Megan, tie her up, and don't do anything more than I tell you to." Mike was hoping that all of Megan's training would help to keep her in line.

Megan bent down and picked up the zip ties. Remembering how much Mike could hurt them, she did what he asked. Allie simply held out her hands, making sure to keep them apart a little, hoping she could slip her hands out when Mike wasn't looking.

"Make sure you tie up her feet too." Mike watched, keeping the gun trained on Allie until she was tied up. He considered Allie to be the greatest threat to his time alone with his family.

"Get back against the wall, Megan." He walked closer to Allie. Pulling out his knife, he placed the gun in the back waistband of his pants. Making sure Allie could see the knife, Mike pulled on the ties to make sure they were tight and secure.

"There. That's how you do it, you stupid cow. Anyone worth their salt would've made sure it was on better than that. You just can't do anything right, can you?"

Mike focused his attention on Megan, who slid down the wall, cringing in anticipation of being hit. She knew what was coming, and Mike wasn't known for being gentle.

Realizing Megan was in shock, Allie decided to speak up. "So, Mike, do you really need a woman like Megan? I mean, what did you ever see in her? What you need is a real woman who would slap you back when you hit her. Someone who isn't afraid to take what you hand out. Or is it that you like the other type of lifestyle better, but you just can't admit it? Does it make you feel like a man's man to hit on someone smaller than you?" Allie questioned, trying to antagonize him.

Instead of growing angry, Mike calmly turned to face Allie. "I'm sure when this is over, there'll be lots of opinions about how I keep my wife in line. I never wanted a man, I like women. Not the bossy kind, but a submissive wife who knows how to learn her lessons. Now Megan here, she stepped over her bounds and showed the whole town I didn't know how to take care of my family responsibilities. When she neglects her responsibilities, she needs a good beating to make sure she won't forget what her duties are. All she had to do was make sure I got home and in bed before half the town saw me. This entire mess could've been avoided if she had just done her job." Mike sounded confident and sure of himself as he ranted on about wifely duties.

Allie was amazed that any man would think a wife was only good for cleaning up his mistakes. When she went to open her mouth, Mike stepped in front of her, tapping her lips with the tip of the knife.

"I'd keep that mouth shut if you don't want me to cut your tongue out. This is between me and my wife, just as it should've been from the beginning." Mike turned to face Megan so he could judge if she was sorry for her actions.

"Megan, honey. I just need to know you're sorry for what you've done, and then we can go somewhere to start over as a family. I know you didn't understand what you were doing to my reputation, but now that you do, I'm sure it won't happen again."

Moving toward Megan, Mike crouched down so that he could see her expression as he trailed the knife along the side of her face. "So, Meg, are you going to apologize so we can get going? I don't want to wait while they get the fire under control."

Megan looked up at Mike. "You bastard. You set a fire so that everyone would be out there trying to save their livelihood, and they wouldn't be able to save us. How could you do that to such innocent people?" Megan had gotten so used to allowing Mike to do whatever he wanted to her, but trying to hurt her new family was a different story.

"Oh, Meg. They're not as innocent as they would have you believe. They're keeping you from me. They're destroying our family by allowing you and Sally to start over without me. What kind of good people would do something like that? Families are supposed to stay together."

"Mike, they're the best family we could ever have asked for because they truly love us. They've helped me get past all the old stuff and start over. Sally has gotten attached to GG and James as grandparents, and she wouldn't want to leave them." Megan's fear of Mike wasn't as strong as the love she had for her new family.

"How dare you call these people family! What, my family wasn't good enough for you? I built our family so we could have a circle of trust. Do you have any idea how much you hurt me when you involved all these people?" Mike stood up and started pacing.

"Really, Megan, I provided for you. I gave you a child and a home. What else could you have possibly needed?" Mike threw the knife at her feet, barely missing her toes. Bending over to retrieve the knife, he grabbed Megan's shoulders instead and started to shake her.

"Why did you need that woman as your friend?" He pointed to Allie. "She's the one that put these ideas in your head. You would've been the perfect wife if she hadn't come around the house, trying to make you into someone you're not. I loved you as my wife." Mike emphasized each sentence with a rough shake that made Megan's teeth clang together loudly.

"That's enough! Stop!" Startled that Allie would say anything to him after his demonstration with the knife, Mike turned to find his daughter standing in the doorway, shouting at him.

Sally was certain her daddy was going to hurt her mommy again, and it was time that he knew it was against the rules.

Mike started to move toward Sally to hug her after weeks without having seen her.

Sally reached out and picked up the gun that was lying on the floor where Allie had left it. "I said stop that, Daddy. You're not going to hurt my mommy again."

"Sally, just put down the gun, honey, before someone gets hurt." Mike started to edge slowly toward her.

Sally backed closer to the doorway so Mike couldn't reach her. "If you come any closer, I'll shoot your knees out. I'm going to make sure you don't ever hurt my mommy again."

Mike stopped to reconsider when Sally readjusted to make sure both hands were holding the gun steady.

"Sweetie, Mommy and I are just having a misunderstanding, that's all."

"Don't lie to me, Daddy, I'm not stupid. I know you hurt my mommy and put her in the hospital. Then you went back to punish her for telling the good police that you were a bully. Bullies get in trouble at school, Daddy. We're supposed to stand up to bullies. You didn't listen to the good police. You hurt Aunt Julie and Aunt Allie, so you're not my daddy anymore. You're the bad police, and you can't hurt my mommy again."

Mike didn't try to argue with her. He just lunged toward Sally, hoping to distract her.

Sally was smarter than he thought and jumped back through the doorway. Aiming at his right knee, she shot the pistol, but she jerked it when she pulled the trigger, causing it to hit his foot instead.

Megan rushed over to Sally and wrapped her tight in a hug. Knowing Mike would take his anger out on Sally, Megan shielded her, leaving her back facing Mike.

Mike was hopping up and down on one foot, muttering, "She shot me. My own kid shot me." Disbelief edged his voice as the blood poured from his foot. Enraged, he took the gun from the back of his pants and aimed it at Megan and Sally.

Feeling betrayed by both mother and daughter, he flicked the safety off.

"Die, you bitches," he shouted, and pulled the trigger.

Hearing the shot, and knowing one of them must have been hit, Megan examined Sally, but didn't see any blood. Hesitating to turn around, she glanced up and saw GG standing just in front of her with a gun pointed straight at Mike.

Sally turned to see what Megan was looking at, and saw GG standing there with blood oozing out of her chest.

"No, G.G! Don't be dead," Sally screamed as she raced to G.G's side as she slid to the floor.

Megan turned to see why Mike had gone silent, only to find him holding his chest. Megan ran to him, kneeling beside him. She could barely hear his raspy voice trying to say something.

"The old lady shot me. First my kid, and then an old lady got the better of me." Mike said the last word in total disbelief.

Megan bent closer so she could whisper in his ear. "I'm so glad she did, because I couldn't have pulled the trigger. I did love you. I just wish I hadn't ever met you. I know you'll get your just rewards where you're going."

Megan got up, leaving Mike gasping at her words and walked over to make sure G. G. was okay.

Allie had managed to scoot over and pick up the knife Mike had dropped when he was shot. Cutting the zip ties from her feet first, she looked at her hands.

"Megan, could you please cut these off me so I can call an ambulance for GG?"

~~~

The next few hours were confusing as the police, paramedics, and firefighters were racing around. There wasn't a chance for it to sink in that Mike was really dead.

Megan had gone to the hospital with GG, while Allie stayed behind to answer questions and help console Sally.

Allie called Justin as soon as the paramedics had GG taken care of, and they were waiting for him to arrive.

The fire had finally been put out, and was in no danger of spreading to the Greenley's other fields.

Justin rushed up to Allie as she sat with Sally on the front porch steps of the main house. Holding onto her as she broke down into tears, Justin realized just how much he loved her.

Minutes later, Allie sniffled and pulled back to look Justin in the face. "I'm okay, but we should take your dad to the hospital and check on your mom."

"I didn't tell him because I didn't want to get into an accident while we were driving back. All he knows is there was a fire and we had to come back." Justin kept his arm around Allie as they went to find his dad.

"Sally, come with us, sweetie. Hop into the truck, and I'm going to get my dad so we can go see GG, okay?" Justin found his dad speaking to a police officer and went to grab him before he found out about GG

Sally was confused because Justin took off before she could answer him.

"It's okay, sweetie. He's just distracted because his mommy is in the hospital. See? He's coming back with Mr. James. Let's go get in the truck." Allie waited for Sally to respond before she went to meet the two men.

"Dad, Mom's in the hospital, but they said she's going to be okay. Come on, I'll drive us to the hospital." He grabbed his dad's arm, pulling him to the truck so they could leave.

Justin was glad to see Allie and Sally in the back seat, ready to go. Mike might be dead, but he didn't want Allie out of his sight.

Justin drove carefully to the ER, since his dad would've been reckless trying to get to his soulmate. They arrived at the hospital a few minutes later in one piece, but before Justin could come to a complete stop, James was out of the vehicle and through the ER doors.

Justin, Allie, and Sally followed at a slower pace, and were told she was still in surgery when they arrived. Heading to the family waiting room, they found Megan. She was wearing scrubs since her clothes had been covered in blood.

Megan hugged James as she apologized. "Oh, Mr. G. I'm so sorry I got her shot. I didn't mean for that to happen. He was aiming at Sally and me, but he hit her instead." Megan burst into tears.

He hugged her back. "Megan, you must quit calling me Mr. G. Just James, or even Dad would be fine. I don't know all the details, Megan, but if GG was there, it was for a good reason. I don't blame you at all, sweetie. We'll get through this, and she'll be all right." James guided her over to the couch and sat them down.

Allie and Justin sat on the couch, with Sally in the middle. Allie was explaining to everyone what had happened when Mark rushed in and came to a complete halt when he saw that Megan and Sally were okay.

"Oh, thank goodness. When the police report came over the scanner, I was in court, and my assistant told me as soon as I got out. All they said was that someone was dead, and one was on the way to the hospital. I was so worried that it was you." Mark walked over and took Megan by the hands and pulled her toward him. He then kissed her. It was one of 'the world is over, and I'm glad you're alive' kind of kiss.

Megan was so shocked, that she sat down and covered her mouth when he was done.

Evidently, Mark had more than a lawyer's interest in Megan's welfare. Allie smirked to herself that there might be romance in the air when things finally calmed down.

Mark looked around and realized everyone but Aunt GG was in the room.

"Oh, no. Uncle James, was Aunt GG the one shot?"

"Yes, and they're removing the bullet and think everything will be okay. So we're just waiting for the doctors to come and update us." James accepted the man hug with a hand slap on the back from his nephew.

Allie went back to the beginning and explained what had happened, with a few helpful words from Sally. Amazingly, Sally seemed unfazed with all the commotion of the day.

They had waited over an hour when the police finally arrived to finish getting the rest of the details and timelines on what had happened back at the ranch.

Taking each one's statement in another room, Megan and Allie were by themselves, but Sally was allowed to have Mark present.

By the time they finished, the doctor had arrived to let them know how GG was doing.

"She had a close miss to her heart, and the bullet was lodged in the top left side of her chest. It wasn't next to anything major, but it took some digging so we wouldn't damage any vital organs around the bullet, but we got it out. She's in recovery right now, and we'll have her in a room shortly. I suggest only one or two close family members at first, then maybe switch out if she's up to it." The doctor knew better then to try and keep all the family out of the room.

Justin and James went in first, while the others waited anxiously outside.

Megan burst into tears of joy when she finally saw GG

"I'm so glad you're okay. I thought we were all going to die. I'm so glad he didn't kill you."

GG wasn't quite recovered, but she knew Megan needed reassurance. "Megan, I walked into that room knowing it was a bad situation. I'm thankful we all got out without more people getting hurt. I'm sorry he died, honey, but it was just an us or him situation. I chose him, so no more tears or worrying. Just go and take good care of Sally. We can talk more when I get out of here."

~~~

After the medical examiner performed the autopsy on Mike, he found there had been two gunshot wounds—one in his foot, the other was the kill shot. It was clearly self-defense since there were four different accounts of the same story as to what he'd done.

They had a simple funeral, with only close family attending. Megan thought a proper funeral would be the best way to bring closure to Sally.

Justin and Allie were thrilled that Mike was no longer a threat, and they could resume their lives. Helping Megan move forward would be the bigger challenge for both of them. They were excited to see how dating under normal circumstances would work out.

Mark was planning to help Megan get settled, and there would be lots of things she needed help with to get everything sorted out in the near future.

Epilogue

Six months later...

"Hey, Stan, where are you? I thought you said there was a flood in here." Confused, Allie started toward the bar until her eyes adjusted from being outside, and then she saw the banner.

Justin followed her in, waiting for her to notice, and got down on one knee. In bold black letters, the banner said, WILL YOU MARRY ME? Right underneath it, in smaller blue letters, were the words AND MY FAMILY?

Turning toward Justin with a look of astonishment, that's when Allie found him down on one knee. "Allie, will you do me the honor of letting me love and protect you? I want to love and cherish you for the rest of your life. Will you marry me?" Justin looked hopeful as he stared up at Allie.

"Yes! Yes! I'll marry you *and* your family." Laughing, Allie looked up and saw the family together, peeking through the partition.

"I think I'll keep all of you, no matter what, if you'll have me?" She gestured for them to come on out and join them.

Sally ran over and jumped into Justin's arms. "I'll marry you, Uncle J, if she ever gets rid of you. I'm next in line." All the adults burst out laughing.

"Sally, I promise if I ever decide to get rid of him, you have first dibs." Allie swung her around in a circle.

"How about this. Since you can't have Justin for a husband, will you settle for being my flower girl?" Allie didn't want Sally to feel left out during the wedding rush.

"Duh. I thought you'd never ask." Sally rolled her eyes at the question, while the adults continued to laugh.

The End

If you would like to shop for beauty products with me go to www.youravon.com/alathiamorgan

Or if you would like to sell www.start.avon.com reference code alathiamorgan

Also the team page is www.facebook.com/AlathiasATeam

If you or someone you know needs help with an abusive or violent situation please get help.

http://www.thehotline.org/ Computer use can be monitored so please use caution when visiting this site.

Or call 1-800-799-7233 | 1-800-787-3224 (TTY)

These are some sites that you may find helpful as well.

Domestic Violence Resource **Center**
www.dvrc-or.org

NRCDV - National Resource **Center on** Domestic Violence
www.nrcdv.org

Domestic Violence Statistics | Domestic Violence Statistics
domesticviolencestatistics.org/**domestic-violence**-stat

Domestic Violence Statistics - **AARDVARC.org**
www.aardvarc.org/dv/**statistics**.shtml

Death by Poison?

Nova Ladies Adventures: Book 2

Needing to rest, Megan realized that she had half an hour before the school bus would bring Sally home. She decided to take a break from cleaning the cabin before her job and role as mommy started. She poured herself a glass of tea and went out to sit on the porch swing.

Enjoying the brief rest during the hot August day, Megan quickly drank her tea and went back inside for a refill. Trying to relax into her new life hadn't been too difficult. Being with Sally made every moment worth all the trouble that her ex-husband, Mike, had ever put her through.

Sitting back on the swing, Megan had trouble relaxing in the stifling 102-degree heat. Gulping down her iced tea, she was hoping it would cool her down, but it wasn't working the way she'd expected.

Feeling that something was wrong, Megan picked up her phone to dial GG, but she had trouble focusing on the screen. Turning to put the glass down on the table next to the swing, she turned too fast, losing her balance. The glass dropped to the table, hitting the edge and tumbling to the floor where it shattered. Megan tried to stop the swing from moving by putting her hand on the wall, which pushed the swing again, overcompensating as she fell to the floor. Her phone flew from her hand, across the porch and out of reach.

Megan didn't know who was trying to kill her now, but was glad that Sally wasn't home to see this happen to her. The fact that she'd been receiving notes all summer had made her cautious, but she hadn't planned to die because of them.

Thankful that she and Sally had a family that accepted them just as they were was wonderful. They could take care of

Sally since what was happening to her right now seemed to be serious. Megan slipped into unconsciousness, her last thoughts of her daughter.

Made in the USA
Columbia, SC
05 February 2018